A Sour Note

by

Jill Piscitello

A Music Box Mystery

A Sour Note

Cover Art by *Jennifer Greeff*

The Wild Rose Press, Inc.
PO Box 708
Adams Basin, NY 14410-0708
Visit us at www.thewildrosepress.com

Publishing History
First Edition, 2023
Trade Paperback ISBN 978-1-5092-4917-6
Digital ISBN 978-1-5092-4918-3

A Music Box Mystery
Published in the United States of America

With his mouth set in a grim line, he waited.

If anyone else had enough nerve to presume she owed them an explanation, she would respond with a solid *mind your own business*. Instead, the seventeen-year-old still inside her refused to tell him to get lost. "He was hiding money in his office." This was one of those times when learning how to wait a few beats before blurting out inflammatory information would come in handy. Each second of passing silence decreased her ability to breathe in the confined space. She turned the ignition and switched on the air-conditioner.

"How do you know?" His volume just above a whisper, each dragged-out word hung in the air.

"I found it."

"When were you in his office?" He swiped at a bead of sweat trickling down the side of his face, then positioned a vent toward him.

"Last night." When would she learn to bite her tongue? Finn's switch from rapid-fire scolding to slow, deliberate questioning left her unable to swallow over the sandpaper lump in her throat.

"Where was Vic?"

She stared at the back of the building, wishing she'd kept her mouth shut. "He'd left for the night." If she averted her gaze, she could pretend his eyeballs weren't bugging out of his head, and his jaw didn't need a crane to haul it off his chest.

"You were at the town hall after hours? Did anyone see you?"

"A custodian opened his door for me." She snuck a glance. Sure enough, features contorted in shock and horror replaced his boy-next-door good looks.

Praise for Jill Piscitello

"A SOUR NOTE introduces a cozy element to the murder mystery genre with increasing suspense, clever plot twists, and a touch of small-town charm."

~Grace P.

~*~

"Jill Piscitello added mystery and suspense from the beginning that kept me intrigued and glued to the book."

~Luwi N.

Dedication

For Rob, Kaelie, and Anthony

Chapter One

Maybe if Maeve waited long enough, they'd go away. How long would someone stand on Mom's front porch knocking and ringing a doorbell before finally giving up? No way would she answer. At almost one o'clock in the afternoon, she still wore her bathrobe and pajamas. All she needed was to give the neighborhood one more thing to say about her present state of mind.

The recent demise of her engagement whispered on everyone's lips. One look at Maeve Cleary and Luanne Fitz and Ida Magee, Hampton Beach, New Hampshire's biggest gossips, would be overcome with a burning need to spread the news about her wallowing in the depths of despair. Anyone unable to dress or run a comb through their hair by midday might recognize the kernel of truth residing in that story. But some things were better left unsaid and unshared.

She sat motionless in the sitting room off the foyer, not daring to make a move toward the stairs lest they glimpse her shadow or spot movement through the frosted side panel windows of the front door. The crunch of gravel announced a car pulling into the driveway, and a door slammed shut. She risked a peek out the bay window.

"Jules," called Luanne's voice. "We've been knocking and knocking. Is Maeve home? Her car's still out front."

"She should be. Can't imagine where she'd go."

The verbal jab to her solar plexus slumped her posture. *Thanks, Mom.* Maeve made a dash for the stairs. She neared the top, three more steps to go, and the front door swung open.

"Maeve," Luanne gasped.

She froze, still not ready to face them.

"If I didn't know better, I'd say you were avoiding us."

The snipping, accusatory tone grated with the same petulance of a whining child. Maeve inhaled a deep breath, plastered on a wide smile, and spun on her toes. Years had passed since she'd last seen Mom's neighbors. Luanne never changed. Her blonde highlights still shimmered, and she'd maintained an apple-shaped figure despite daily walks. At sixty-four years old, the petite, five-foot-four stature and few extra pounds kept her features soft and youthful. In sharp contrast, Ida dyed her hair a shade too dark. The cut, color, and rail-thin frame aged her a good ten years. "Never, Luanne. What a silly thing to say." With acute longing, she glanced up the last few steps. "I-I spilled coffee on my blouse earlier." She gestured toward her ensemble and aimed for a carefree pose with the other hand on her hip. "Hence the robe. I was just running upstairs to pull my top out of the dryer."

"Why not put on something else?" asked Ida.

Instead of asking why Ida couldn't mind her own business, she bit her tongue and forced another smile. "I had my heart set on wearing blue today."

"Oooh, going someplace special?" asked Jules. As she clasped her hands together, the bangle bracelets on both wrists jangled. Even a short errand required jewelry and a pair of heels for Mom. Minimal makeup enhanced the same, fine-featured bone structure she shared with Maeve.

The desperate lilt in Mom's voice, conveying hope her daughter had found a reason to leave the house after hibernating for five consecutive days, sparked a flicker of guilt. "Special? No." The cobwebbed recesses of her foggy brain failed to produce a destination to appease the three women standing in the foyer.

Incapable of fully comprehending Maeve's misfortune, Luanne and Ida knew the joys of wonderful marriages to husbands who adored them and children who appeared to do no wrong. Heavy on the *appeared*. Maeve grew up with those now-adult children and knew firsthand the mischief they'd gotten into and the mistakes they'd made, even if their parents remained, to this day, blissfully unaware. "Thought I'd go for a walk and see if anything's changed on the boardwalk. I'd better get going before this beautiful summer day passes me by." Maeve pivoted and tripped over one of Mom's five cats before jogging to the second-floor landing. After racing up the few stairs, she rounded the corner, ducked into her bedroom, closed the door, and face-planted on the four-poster double bed.

The prospect of remaining in the room all day and forgoing food and water appealed to her recent proclivity for avoiding other humans. But after allowing herself a mere two minutes to wallow, she shifted to a sitting position and rested her gaze on the towering, custom dollhouse she still adored. Unfortunately, none of the perfect stories she'd created under that hip roof colonial panned out in real life.

Maybe a walk wasn't such a bad idea. Sure, anyone

who crossed her path would know the gory details of her widely publicized tale of romantic woe. But she refused to let Greyson Walker's disgusting behavior dictate one more minute of her life. He did her a favor. Better to see his true colors revealed now rather than later. If only she possessed a humiliation off switch.

Minutes later, Luanne's and Ida's animated goodbyes pealed up the stairs and through her closed door. Maeve padded to the bench seat nestled in her turret window. Outside, the two women power-walked onto the sidewalk. Both clad in designer athleisure, they personified workout chic. Neither of their taut ponytails dared allow a stray wisp to slip from their elastics.

Another chance to escape might not present itself before more of Jules's well-meaning, yet prying, friends dropped by. After changing into the least wrinkled items piled in a heap on her floor and stuffing a ten-dollar bill in her pocket, she hollered a goodbye, yanked open the front door, and bounded down the porch steps into the welcoming July heat.

"When do you think you'll be back?" Hanging out a second-floor bedroom window, Mom's pink-tipped silver locks glinted in the sunlight. "I thought we'd go to dinner tonight with Calista. My treat."

The mention of her cousin's name set her temples throbbing. For a single woman living alone, Mom's house saw more people coming and going than some small hotels. Better to join them for dinner, then escape to the sweet seclusion of her room for the remainder of the night. Her hand did little to shield the glare from the sun. "I won't be gone for more than an hour or two. Dinner sounds great."

"Leave yourself time to change your clothes. You

can borrow something from my closet." Without waiting for a response, Jules closed the window.

Maeve continued to squint at the two-story beach house awash with windows offering a panoramic view of the Atlantic Ocean. She had to hand it to the woman. Single-handedly maintaining the pristine condition of the stunning interior, exterior, and landscaping of this property required diligence and a keen eye for detail. Mom tended to the upkeep of her home with the same attention reserved for her personal well-being and appearance.

One glance down at her outfit reflected proof that, sometimes, the apple did fall far from the tree. What was wrong with shorts and a plain, white T-shirt? Many people would define this outfit as a classic look. The old ketchup stain along the shirt's hem was barely noticeable. And sure, the baggy denim sagged around her slim hips in a rather unflattering manner. But the blame for her recent weight loss rested solely on Greyson's shoulders.

Granted, her hair had its limitations. On better days, someone might describe the style as voluminous. Well, if someone had a way with words and was being kind. Today was not one of those days, so she'd swept the dry, staticky strands into a bun. Was it her fault if the result fell more in the realm of the literal meaning of the word messy than the whimsical, wispy updo she'd aimed for? Everyone had their limitations. Styling her limp, perpetually frayed locks was a battle conceded long ago.

Sucking in a fortifying gulp of air, she rested both hands on the small of her back and allowed her lungs to fully expand. With her chest filled to overflowing, she released the breath in a controlled whoosh and set off in search of something cool and sweet to drink while the warm sand soothed her soul.

The mile-and-a-half scenic coastal path never grew old. Other than venturing onto Mom's deck overlooking the ocean, she stayed inside. But as she approached the bustling boardwalk, the ninety-degree temperature seeping into her bones and the echo of waves lapping to shore offered a small measure of comfort. For a moment, she paused and leaned against the sea wall with eyes closed and allowed the salty air to wash over her while the music and voices faded into a blurred background din.

No one kicked off summer like this town. After a deep intake and release of breath, she strolled toward the sand sculptures lining a section of beach. The sculpting competition was held weeks ago, but the meticulous works of art remained intact in astonishing detail. Suddenly parched, she stopped and stared at the strip of gift shops, ice cream stands, restaurants, and open-air take-out windows offering everything from pizza to sushi. The throngs of people milling about and waiting in lines deposited a leaden weight of anxiety on her chest. Instead of picking up a much-desired fresh lemonade, she headed for home.

With the hubbub left behind, she sighed, her shoulders relaxing. As the meditative hum of the surf drowned out car engines passing by, she slowed her pace. Priscilla's Pin Cushion stood on the corner of Ocean Boulevard and Arbor Way. Images flashed of the endless hours spent getting sized for alterations to costumes and prom gowns. A car door slammed in front of the shop and jolted Maeve into the present.

The person sitting in the driver's side of a gleaming red convertible gesticulated with flailing arms.

Whoever was on the receiving end of that tirade deserved a heaping dose of pity. Dwelling on someone else's misery wouldn't ease her own. Besides, she could do with an iced coffee and made a beeline for Happy Beans. As she opened the painted white door and stepped inside, she was enveloped by the familiar scent of a rich medley of brews. The exquisite aroma almost made up for the frigid air blasting from a nearby vent. Little had changed in the past decade. Several tables stood on both sides of the coffee shop. Not more than fifty people could dine at one time, but the few bistro tables lining the sidewalk allowed for overflow. As usual, customers occupied most of the seats inside. A hum of voices welcomed her and brought to mind lazy summer afternoons spent sipping cool, coffee concoctions after hours of soaking up the sun. To her delight, the path to the register was empty.

"Am I hallucinating, or did a ghost just walk into my coffee shop?"

She slid her gaze to the far-left corner of the café.

Finn Keaton stood before the swinging door to the kitchen.

The same Finn Keaton she'd dropped like a hot potato on her way to fame and fortune. On this occasion, Mom deserved a nod for the ill-received beauty advice she'd doled out over the years. Less than an hour ago, her casual outfit was an acceptable choice for a stroll into town. Now, the sloppy clothes in conjunction with the frizzing top knot sporting dark roots begging for a foil and fingernails with peeled, not chipped, polish failed Wardrobe Attire for Bumping into an Ex-Boyfriend 101.

Thanks to a reflex born from years of near-daily visits, she gallivanted into the coffee shop without a second thought. Here she wouldn't have to brave the crowds streaming along the boardwalk. Instead, a worse fate waited. One with russet hair always in need of a trim, heavily lashed copper eyes, and a slim build. The man had barely changed in a decade. Every muscle in her body stiffened.

Finn's face broke into an enormous, toothy grin. "I'm teasing you. Get over here and pull up a stool."

Only an air raid siren had a hope of drowning out the pounding of her heart. Straightening her spine, she strode toward the counter. "Tell me you have some of your dad's famous chocolate brownie brew on tap. Medium, iced, and to go, please."

He nodded and stepped toward the rear counter. After filling a cup with ice, he glanced over his shoulder, then reached for one of the coffeepots. "What brings you back to town?" Placing a cap on top, he faced her and slid the cup across the counter.

"You honestly haven't heard?" She tugged a straw from a dispenser that sat next to the register longer than she'd been alive, removed the paper wrapper, and popped the straw into the cup.

With one eyebrow raised, he rested both forearms on the counter. "Word does spread fast around here, but one never knows how much truth remains in a story by the time it reaches one's ears."

She wrapped both hands around the plastic cup already beading with condensation and shrugged. "Whatever you've heard is probably true."

"In that case, your coffee's on the house." He

gestured over her shoulder. "Paige is over there. I don't think she saw you come in."

Maeve craned her neck and gazed past a table full of construction workers. Her oldest and dearest friend, Paige Walsh, sat at a corner window with her back to the room. A glimpse of earbuds peeking through long, golden strands of hair explained why she bebopped in her chair to a tune unheard by anyone else.

When Maeve left town, their friendship didn't miss a beat for the first few years. But after she started dating Greyson, they lost touch. Not completely, but noticeably. The occasional brief text message replaced hours spent chatting on the phone and long weekend trips to New York.

As she stared across the café, she couldn't ignore the pang of loss settling in her stomach. Paige's job as a voice teacher at Jules's music school, The Music Box, was one of the few threads still connecting their lives. Mom served as a messenger, sharing most details of her oldest friend's life. She faced Finn and sipped. The cool, chocolatey liquid, closer to dessert than coffee, slid down her throat. "As delicious as I remember. Thank you for a much-needed dose of caffeine. I'm going over to say hello."

After maneuvering through the obstacle course of chairs blocking her path and customers leaving, she stopped in front of Paige's table. "Paige?" No response. Earbuds definitely blocked all other sounds. A tap on the shoulder might startle her. She rounded the table and sat. Still no response. Cascades of honey waves bounced around her heart-shaped face. Paige still favored an early '60s vibe with a wide headband matching her yellow shift dress. Maeve stretched an arm across the table and shielded the phone screen with a hand.

One glance sent Paige lurching back. With a shriek, she yanked out the earbuds, leapt out of her seat, and threw both arms around Maeve.

The five-foot-two woman's bear hug combined with a lengthy, piercing squeal knocked her off balance.

After releasing her grip, Paige dropped onto the chair and thrust both hands in the air. "I texted and called you several times. I've been contemplating whether or not I should show up at your house uninvited."

"Sorry." Her chest tightened. More than once over the last week, she'd crafted and deleted several replies to Paige's messages. But she didn't want a pep talk. She wanted to wallow. Mom had her faults, but she knew and respected how Maeve processed upsets. All good intentions aside, Paige's sunny outlook was better suited to minor setbacks than major life upheavals scrutinized by a national audience. "I needed a few days to screw my head on straight." Probing mahogany eyes saw more than the unkempt hair and sloppy clothing. As if she needed more evidence a smidgen of effort into her appearance was in order.

"Looks like you're about halfway there. Finn should have given you a bagel to go with that coffee." She wrinkled her nose and flicked a hand up and down. "I think I gained the ten or so pounds you've lost."

"It suits you."

"I know." A smirk twitched at the corners of her mouth. "How long are you here?"

"I haven't gotten that far."

"Well, I need to get over to The Music Box." Paige

drifted her gaze toward the hand-carved cuckoo clock hanging over the breakfast bar. "I have an appointment in a half hour. Walk with me?" She stood and slipped her phone into a dainty, black, patent leather handbag better suited for someone closer to Grandma Calliope's age.

Maeve waved and flashed a smile toward Finn, grabbed her coffee, and followed Paige outside. Free from the torture of his air-conditioner, she embraced the blast of warmth and picked up her pace to keep in step.

"I hope you'll be in town for a short while at least. We have a lot to catch up on. You know Ryan got engaged?" As always, Paige walked as fast as she spoke.

"Yeah, you told me a while back." Keeping up with Paige's near-jogging pace made it impossible to read her expression. But her past with Ryan was enough for Maeve to envision the tiny line creasing above her left eyebrow. Although they transitioned to a platonic relationship years ago, Paige assessed his subsequent girlfriends with the same discerning eye usually reserved for parents determining whether or not someone was good enough for their child. "Are you still not a fan of his fiancée?"

"That woman. She's…She's…" She shook her head and groaned.

"That bad?"

"If truth be told, I should cut her some slack. Staying engaged to a man who remains close friends with his ex can't be easy. But the fact we've been in the friend zone for over ten years has zero impact on her insecurity."

More breathless than a thirty-five-year-old woman

should be, Maeve rested a firm palm on the cramp forming in her side. "I see why your history might bother her."

"Our history isn't the problem." Paige stopped in front of The Music Box, rooted in her purse, and fished out a key. "She's not a nice person. I can't quite put my finger on it, but her presence reeks of something sneaky. And she's cold."

Please let this not be a loaded question. "Are you sure the issue doesn't have something to do with old feelings resurfacing?"

Rolling her eyes, Paige unlocked the door. "Don't go there. We were kids."

Maeve flipped the light switch, dashed inside, and twirled in a circle with arms spread wide and head thrown back. "Home sweet home!" she crowed. Eyes damp, she stopped and dropped her hands. "I always did love spending time here." Her earliest memories drifted between the beach house and Mom's music school. The countless yet enjoyable hours with staff and clientele created a child who, by the age of five, interchanged references to her mother as Jules and Mom to fit the conversation.

Impressive updates were made since she'd last been inside the school. Shelves of used instruments available for resale now lined buttercream walls once home to a variety of tattered posters. Only the occasional, well-thought-out framed picture hung in the few available spaces. Gleaming gray-toned, wood laminate flooring replaced the well-worn linoleum. An ornate, antique desk sat in the far corner of the room with a hot-pink accent chair more befitting an English manor home than a music school. A variety of instruments filled the room, including a sleek black, baby grand piano. White French doors at the back of the room provided a glimpse of the space used for voice lessons. A delicate chandelier dangled from the center of the ceiling, tying together a theme of music and elegance.

"Jules did a stunning job redecorating, didn't she?" Paige asked. "Soak it all in quickly because Trixie'll be here any minute. You can judge her for yourself."

"What?" Maeve darted her gaze toward the entrance. "Why is she coming here?"

"She's my appointment. Miss Trixie Bell is now a student at The Music Box. She signed up for voice lessons so she can serenade Ryan at the wedding."

In an obvious effort to fit in as many words as possible before Trixie arrived, Paige rambled on at warp speed without taking a breath.

"Just another way for the bride-to-be to ensure everyone's staring at her at all times." Both hands clutched her chest. "I've never met another soul who craves attention like her."

"And now *I'll* have the pleasure of making her acquaintance. Sounds like a real treat." Maeve strolled the perimeter of the room and stopped in front of an antique violin hanging on the wall. "After you told me about the engagement, I checked out a few of her social media outlets. She has quite the fan base."

"She certainly does. Online, she's a social media darling simply *bursting* with smiles and sweet gestures. The woman is always running some promotional giveaway or promoting a charitable venture that never fails to benefit *her* in some way. Last month, she convinced her fans to mail teddy bears for her to personally deliver to local pediatric wards. Sounds like she has a heart of gold, right?" She snorted. "Wrong. The event cost a few dollars in gas money and two hours out of her day. She stood for photo ops outside the hospitals and then dumped the bears at nurses' stations without even spending ten minutes with any of those kids."

"But how do you—"

Paige lifted a finger and sank onto a silver stool. "And I know this fact because I have friends who work at two of the hospitals. The following day, she released a video advertising her online fashion consulting services and couldn't keep up with the demand." She stood again and paced with her hands doing as much of the talking as her mouth. "I know I sound petty. I'm sure those kids were beyond happy to get the bears. I just don't agree with presenting yourself as a saint for the sole purpose of self-promotion. That's not the same thing as being a good person."

"I get it. And I don't think you're petty. She's pretending to be someone she's not all the way to the bank." Maeve dragged her fingertips across the smooth surface of a music stand.

With a frown forming, Paige stopped and stared out the front window. "Here comes the selfie queen now."

A stunning woman glided inside. Glossy, jet-black hair fell to her waist. Heavily fringed, wide emerald eyes took up most of a face best described as sun-kissed. A strappy sundress prominently showcasing bronzed shoulders and toned legs teetering on a gleaming pair of pink heels defined the summer season. Did she have somewhere to be after the lesson, or does she leave her house looking like a supermodel every day?

Trixie fixed her gaze on Paige. "Am I walking into a scheduling mix-up? Daphne swore you had this half hour free today."

"Don't worry." She held up a hand with an open palm. "This is my friend Maeve. She's not here for a lesson. We came from grabbing a cup of coffee."

Bristling at the woman's clipped tone, Maeve slapped on a smile and approached with a hand outstretched. "I'm so excited to meet you. I hear you're marrying one of my oldest friends."

"Maeve?" She accepted but didn't return the handshake. "I don't recall Ryan mentioning you."

"I live in New York now, and I'm sorry to say we've lost touch over the years. But once upon a time, a small group of us spent nearly every free minute together." A critical gaze flicked over Maeve, sizing her up in a heartbeat. And…dismissed.

Trixie brushed past Paige with hips swaying far more than necessary. "Let's get started. I'm not paying you to stand around chatting with your friend, and I have errands to run after my lesson." As if born on a runway, she strutted toward the French doors and entered the voice room.

At Paige's see-what-I-mean look, Maeve pursed her lips. "I think I'll pop over to Dog Eared and pick up a few used books to occupy my time while I'm home."

"I'll meet you after the lesson."

"Okay." Once outside, she sucked in a breath at the regret seizing her chest. She should have used her exit as an opportunity to go home. Although the thought of returning to the privacy of her bedroom loomed like a glorious beacon of hope, she shook her head. Paige would welcome a friendly face and an ear after spending thirty minutes gnawing on her tongue.

The stroll to the bookstore eased some of the tension radiating through her body. How did Ryan get himself tangled up with that toxic woman? In under ten minutes, she managed to permeate The Music Box with a suffocating cloud of negativity. As a list of choice adjectives for Trixie grew, she paused. The raven-haired diva wasn't the true source of her stress.

For the first time in almost five days, she left Mom's property. Neighborhood visitors were bad enough. But after a public scandal left her ditched at the altar and destitute, she couldn't shed the ball of lead from the pit of her stomach. A root canal was more appealing than the prospect of facing the entire town. While tourist season came and went, a close-knit group of year-round locals remain in the neighborhood, intertwined with each other's lives.

When Maeve began dating Greyson Walker, the famous news correspondent on a nationally broadcasted morning show, residents in Hampton gobbled every tidbit Mom was willing to share and every tabloid article they could get their hands on. Rich, handsome, and famous, he checked more boxes than the women of Clover Lane knew what to do with. The engagement announcement resulted in behaviors more appropriate to expectations of a royal wedding invitation.

Last weekend, those plans went up in smoke along with the interior of Greyson's sports car. He'd been sneaking around with Shannen Plum, America's wannabe movie sweetheart. Wannabe failed to achieve national adoration because she was more famous for getting publicly plastered than for box office hits.

The rumor mill spread a tale of an intoxicated Shannen lighting matches while Greyson drove them home from a concert. Who can imagine why she decided to play with fire that night? Inebriated, she dropped a lit match, and impaired reflexes prevented her from finding it before the napkins scattered on the floor caught fire.

Every time she rode in his car, Maeve complained about those napkins sticking to her heels. Nothing dressed down an outfit like paper products trailing from one's shoes. Turned out Greyson's propensity to collect trash wasn't limited to inanimate objects.

In the end, the small fire and resulting fender bender paled in comparison to the ensuing catastrophe which occurred when witnesses pulled over to help and started snapping pictures of Greyson and Shannen. Those pictures went viral, and Maeve went home to hide.

As she ambled along Arbor Way, she met casual greetings with a smile. But passersby expressions not so subtly masking raised eyebrows and hushed gossip indicated inevitable stares and questions didn't disappear simply because she did. People in town were entitled to their curiosity. But her fragile nerves left her more unprepared than she'd expected. Had she emerged from her self-induced exile too soon?

Chapter Two

Maeve stared at the hundred-plus-year-old farmhouse and leaned into the calming sensation sweeping over her. As a child, Dog Eared was her sanctuary. She'd spent countless hours lapping up the quiet solitude while devouring book after book by the floor to ceiling stone fireplace. She hadn't intended to come here today but was now grateful for the idea. Having something to read during her stay might be nice.

After forty minutes spent perusing the aisles, she balanced three novels in one arm and strained to reach a fourth on the top shelf. Just as her hand gripped the book, the others tumbled to the floor. She fell into the bookcase and failed to catch the rainfall of literature. Instead, several more novels plummeted to the ground.

Paige rounded the corner and giggled. "No one ever described you as graceful before. Perhaps no one ever will."

"Keep your compliments to yourself, and help me put the aisle back together before they ban me for life."

Paige stooped to assist. "So, what did you think of Trixie?"

"I only spent five seconds with her but can't for the life of me imagine what Ryan sees in that woman. She's like a beautiful ice queen."

"Oh, she fawns all over him and makes him feel

like he's king of the world." She slid a book into place, lifted an index finger, and quirked up one side of her mouth in a grimace. "Everyone else she treats like dirt. But she's smart enough to avoid revealing her superior attitude in front of him."

Maeve stood and tossed her head to the side, but stray strands still drifted into her eyes. "Have you said anything?"

"Once, but my opinion wasn't well received."

With the shelf in order, Maeve retrieved her original selections. "I'd better check out before risking another mess. Hey, Mom and I are going to dinner tonight. You should join us. We can continue this topic over a plate of calamari. You know my mom would love to be part of the discussion."

Full dimples bloomed on Paige's cheeks. "I'd love to." She narrowed her gaze. "I know that face. What aren't you telling me?"

Just once, Maeve would like a mirror handy for one of these so called "faces" Paige never failed to recognize. Did withholding information result in an involuntary eye twitch or lip sneer she wasn't aware of? "My cousin Calista is coming into town tonight and is staying at my mom's for a week."

Paige jerked back her head and blinked, but the hint of a smile touched her lips. "Not Creepy Calista?"

"The one and only. She's in town for the Botanical Benefits Expo." She shrugged. "I haven't seen her since we were kids. Maybe she's not creepy anymore."

"Keep telling yourself that. But I'll still come."

"Unless you need to go home first, we can go to my mom's now." Sidestepping a group of children gathered on the floor with a slew of picture books,

Maeve headed for the cashier. "She was quite anxious I make myself presentable before going out."

"Is that your subtle way of saying you want me to do something with your hair?" With a half grin, she lifted an eyebrow.

An unladylike snort burst out. "Want and need are two very different things. No one has ever tamed my mop better." Paige began performing at the age of five. The quick changes that accompany theater and beauty pageants inadvertently created a skilled hairdresser and makeup artist capable of gorgeously transforming anyone who crossed her path.

"Facts. I'll need to charge my phone." She dipped a hand into her purse, then rifled through at a more frantic pace. A deep sigh slumped her shoulders. "I must have left my phone over at The Music Box. I'll run back and meet you at your mom's in a bit."

With a thud, Maeve dropped her reading selections onto the counter. "I walked here. So, I'll tag along, and you can drive us both."

Less than ten minutes later, Maeve crossed Arbor Way. Nearing the music school, she pointed toward the door. "Hey, I don't think you locked up."

"Of course, I did." At once, Paige stopped short and gaped at the door. "Maybe Jules stopped by."

Despite the doubt threatening to hold her back, Maeve shoved open the door and entered the school. One glance darted to the left provided credence for Paige's theory. "The alarm's disabled. Mom?" She stepped farther into the room. Shuffling feet sounded under the reception desk. A slight unease settled itself in her stomach.

"Nope. Just me." A tall, lanky redhead heaved

himself off the floor.

"Seamus!" As she rushed forward, she couldn't keep the girlish squeal from escaping her lips.

He stepped out from behind the desk and swept her off the ground.

"Look at you." When her feet set on the floor, she gave him the once-over. "Where's the little boy I used to know and adore?"

Soon after turning twelve, Maeve began babysitting her neighbor Seamus. He'd been four years old at the time, and they forged an immediate bond. She babysat for the family until Seamus's own twelfth birthday declaration he could fend for himself for a few hours. An image of her chasing after him along the salt marsh behind his house flashed before her eyes. His backyard brimming with stepping-stones, a footbridge, wildflowers, and ducks made for endless adventures.

"Oh, he's still in here somewhere." He laughed and tapped his chest.

"What were you doing under the desk?"

"Your mom asked me to come over and take a look at the computer." His face reddened under a smattering of brown freckles. "From what I've been told, this outdated machine's been causing some headaches."

"You can say that again." Paige jabbed a finger toward the hulking desktop. "The thing's a flippin' dinosaur."

"Seriously. If she holds onto the unit for a few more years, she could auction it off as an antique." He slid a hand into his pocket and withdrew a set of keys. "Since you're here, would you return the keyring to your mom?"

"Sure." The keys landed in her open palm with a

satisfying clink. "Are you finished?"

"Yeah, not that I did much." He zipped a backpack and slung it over his shoulder. "She'll need a replacement soon."

"I'll pass on the message, but she'll probably want to talk to you herself."

"Okay. I've got to get going." He gave her another quick hug. "It was great to see you."

"You, too."

He headed for the door but stopped and spun on his heel. "Hey, who left a cell phone on the baby grand?"

"That'd be mine," Paige called after him.

"I should've guessed." Chuckling, he left.

"Har, har." As she grabbed the phone, a smirk tugged at the corners of Paige's mouth.

After double-checking the lock on the front entrance, Maeve exited through the back door and followed Paige into the parking lot toward her car.

"Ugh. I'm sorry. Let me get these out of your way." A pile of snacks, clothes, and trash loomed on the front seat. She unlocked the passenger door and flung jackets, shoes, and sweaters into a backseat already bursting with similar items.

Someone hasn't conquered her tendency toward procrastination. Though neat as a pin from head to toe, the woman thought nothing of accumulating a landfill's worth of junk in her car. Maeve opened the rear door and gathered an empty pizza box, several crumpled bags, and a coffee cup. "I'll drop these in the dumpster." She bumped the car door closed with a hip and made her way to the rear of the building. The precarious tower of trash in her arms threatened to tip over.

Gingerly balancing the items in one hand while lifting the top of the dumpster, she stood on her toes and leaned forward. As the trash tumbled in, a pink patent leather pump peeked through.

"Hold that lid." Paige skittered across the parking lot carrying the remnants of more food wrappers and containers in both hands. "Geesh, I'm already sweating like a pig."

Did she ever eat a meal outside of her car? Another heap crashed into the dumpster.

"Hey, is that a heel?" Paige tilted her head and peered inside.

"Looks like a waste of a cute pair of shoes." The lid slammed shut.

"No, it looks like Trixie's shoe." On tiptoes, Paige used one hand to hoist herself up while the other lifted the dumpster lid open again. "I swear she builds outfits around those things. You must have noticed them today." After a quick scan, she lowered herself and stepped back. "Keep that thing open."

Easy for her to say. For someone adverse to upper body workouts, Maeve's arms burned.

Seconds after disappearing behind the dumpster, Paige resumed her position with a stick in hand. "You're taller." She thrust the stick at Maeve. "Push a few things around and look for the other one."

"Why do you care if Trixie got sick of her shoes?"

She bit her lip. "I don't."

With the stick outstretched, Maeve leaned farther inside. She swept from left to right and sifted through papers, boxes, and remnants of fabric. "What's with all that glitter? Someone tossed an awful lot of scraps of material in here."

"Those were Priscilla's." Paige boosted herself higher. "I bumped into her last night and found her fuming about ordering fabric for a dress. The quality of material turned out to be super cheap. Not a big surprise, considering she bought a final sale item." With a grunt, she dropped to the ground. "She said years will go by before all the glitter disappears from her shop. I don't know what the big deal is; not much waste is inside here."

"What's in the way?" As Maeve posed the question, she swept the stick, jostling the original shoe and revealed the bottom of a foot. "Is that a—" She swallowed, unable to form another word.

Paige peered over her shoulder and gasped. "A foot?" She grabbed Maeve's arm, digging her nails into the skin.

Maeve shrugged off her vise-like grip and nudged aside random items until the body emerged. A woman with a gleaming head of black hair fanned out around her lay sprawled facedown. Glitter stuck to her bare arms and legs.

A wave of nausea rose up Maeve's throat. This morning's iced coffee threatened to spew forth. She choked on a gag reflex.

"Trixie?" Paige grabbed the stick from Maeve and poked the motionless figure's shoulder. "Trixie!"

"Move away from her," rasped Maeve. "I'll call the police."

****

Seven eternal minutes later, the parking lot blazed with sirens blaring and lights flashing. A swarm of police officers emerged from their cars.

Several yards away, Maeve sat on the ledge of a

cement window, gripping Paige's clammy hand. The sun beat down, leaving her lightheaded. Without the slightest relief of shade and jelly for legs, she didn't dare stand without support.

A hulking man strode across the asphalt. "Are you the ones who called?"

Maeve nodded, every nerve ending on fire. He didn't need a uniform to let her know he was a police officer. The steady eye contact, set jaw, and confident posture provided more clues than a flashed badge. Grandpa, former chief of police, held the same air of authority until his last breath. Close-cropped black hair intensified glinting blue eyes set against a tawny complexion she suspected was quite fair in the cooler seasons. "My mom owns The Music Box. She's on her way."

"I'm Detective Taylor. I'll need you two to stay here. Once we're finished inside, we'll have some questions for you. When your mom arrives, please ask her to do the same." He jotted down their names and gestured to an officer nearby. "That's Officer O'Brien. Let him know if you need anything."

No niceties or inquiries to how they might be doing, Detective Taylor stalked away, leaving no doubt Officer O'Brien's sole purpose was to ensure she didn't budge from her current spot. The poor man's beet-red face begged for a reprieve from the heat.

"Maeve!"

She whipped her head toward the shrill voice.

On kitten heels, Jules jogged down the side alley and struggled to catch her breath. "What on earth?" she panted. "The police set up a roadblock, and I had to park out front. What is going on?"

Although the trembling ceased, an overwhelming weakness glued her to the ledge. "We don't have all the details yet. When they're finished inside, the police want to talk to us. Maybe they'll tell us what happened to Trixie."

Mom's professionally manicured eyebrows shot to her hairline. "Are we supposed to just sit around here twiddling?"

"Yeah, I think so." If Jules wanted to argue that fact, she could confront the detective. But she better not expect backup. That guy didn't look like someone who appreciated anyone getting in his way.

Jules darted her gaze between Maeve and Paige. "Well, one or both of you better start filling me in now on the little information you do have."

On the verge of responding, Maeve closed her mouth at the sight of Finn heading in their direction.

"Everything okay?" Though he stood beside Maeve, his gaze scanned the parking lot, swarming with police, paramedics, camera crews, and bystanders watching the action.

Chances were good that Trixie's death would hit him harder than the rest of them, if for no other reason than she was engaged to his best friend. That fact, combined with his tendency to befriend anyone who crossed his path, forced her to pause and invoke what she hoped was a soft tone. *Still, he'll find out soon enough.* "No. We found a dead body." How did those words just leave her mouth?

"That Trixie Bell. No one knows how to create problems quite like that woman." A light sheen of perspiration shone on Jules's forehead.

"Trixie? What does she have to do with this

situation?" Gaping, Finn straightened.

"I wish we knew." Paige wrapped her arms around her midsection. "Not much more than an hour ago, she was complaining and barking orders, as usual."

"So, she was here for her voice lesson?" Squeezing her eyes closed, Jules pinched the bridge of her nose. With her posture sagging, she sighed and dropped her hand. "I could barely follow what Maeve said on the phone."

"Yeah. After the session, she didn't waste any time leaving." Paige lifted a hand and made a "stop" motion with her palm. "Not that Trixie ever made a habit of engaging in friendly small talk. After she left, I locked up and met Maeve at Dog Eared."

"Has anyone reached out to Ryan?" asked Finn.

Unshed tears shone in Paige's eyes. "How are we supposed to deliver this news?" She swiped at the single drop spilling onto her cheek. "By now, the police have probably contacted him."

"I'll give him a call." Finn rested a hand on Maeve's arm. "But first, can I get you ladies anything while you're waiting? I can run back to the café and grab some drinks or food."

She shook her head. Any semblance of an appetite evaporated by the unexpected turn of events. "Thanks, anyway." She dredged up a small smile. For what felt a century, but was closer to thirty minutes, she sat in uncomfortable silence, watching the activity of people entering and exiting the music school. Seeing Detective Taylor approach again, she swayed with the surging thud of her heart, praying he'd have some answers. But his grim expression deposited a brick of dread on her chest.

"Would you ladies mind joining me at the station?"

"I have my car." The color drained from Paige's face as she clutched her throat and swallowed. "But I don't think I could focus on the road right now."

"Let's take my car," Finn said. "When you're ready, I'll drive you back here."

"I couldn't ask you to close the café." Maeve swallowed. Her throat was sandpaper dry. She should have let him grab some water bottles.

"You didn't. My niece is holding down the fort right now and can handle the customers 'til closing." He glanced at his watch. "We're only open another hour and a half."

Jules squeezed his arm.

"Make a decision, and let's get going. I have a long night ahead." Detective Taylor stalked to his waiting car.

Chances were, they had a draining evening ahead, as well.

****

After a lengthy interview and another half hour waiting for the officers to finish with Mom and Paige, Maeve was free to go. Shaken and famished, she exited the police station on wobbly limbs. In the early evening air, a cool breeze blew through her light T-shirt. She climbed into Finn's car, turned off the air-conditioner, and collapsed against the seat with eyes closed. As the car traveled along the road, the purr of the engine quieted her rattled nerves.

"I know greasy spoons aren't included in your usual haunts, Jules. But I'm making a pit stop at Becky's Barn for some sustenance." Finn steered into a parking spot. "The food is good, and service is quick.

You three don't look like you'll do much better than one of Becky's beef sandwiches tonight."

At the sight of the rustic red barn and the scent of fried food wafting into the car, Maeve swooned. "No arguments here." With one click, she unbuckled her seatbelt and looked over her shoulder. "Mom, have you talked to Calista?"

"Briefly. I told her she'd be on her own for dinner tonight. She knows where the spare key is."

At least one of today's headaches was taken care of. The mere prospect of making small talk with a long-lost cousin she'd never had an ounce in common with further depleted her fading energy.

Once ensconced on the expansive rear deck in a booth with bags of sandwiches, fries, cole slaw, and a tray of drinks, she dug in. Not even the sunset view of the marsh or the relentless caws of pleading seagulls drew her attention. For several minutes, only the rustling of wrappers and the occasional sigh of gratitude was uttered at their table. By some miracle, the onion rings dripping with grease held onto a crispy batter that melted in the mouth.

Paige nibbled on a french fry. "They think I killed her." Her words were just above a whisper.

At the genuine despair resonating in Paige's voice, Maeve inhaled, and the blood coursing through her veins stood still. She lifted a hand to cover her mouth, but instead reached across the table and gripped Paige's forearm. "That's a ridiculous thing to say."

"Not true." As she pulled her arm away, her chin quivered. With glassy eyes, she shook her head. "I was the last one to see her alive."

"That we know of." Finn rose from the booth and

29

grabbed a saltshaker from a nearby table.

"Still." Paige took a miniscule bite of her cheeseburger and chewed.

"What's your motive?" asked Jules. "Her terrible voice drove you to madness?"

Paige's burger landed on the plate with a thud, scattering ketchup and pickles onto the table. With whitening knuckles, she clenched a napkin and twisted. "Try she's marrying my old boyfriend, and they think I'm a jealous ex."

Even if no one wanted to admit it, she had a point. "Where is Ryan anyway?" asked Maeve. "I'm surprised we didn't see him at the station."

"I don't know. Trixie didn't say anything to me." Paige sipped her soda, the ice cubes rattling. "That should have been a red flag. I don't think I've ever had a single interaction with her when she didn't find some sweet gesture of his to tell me about. She always made sure I was good and informed about his devotion."

"Don't worry about it." Jules patted her hand. "When the police start digging, they'll learn quite a few people disliked her."

"Doesn't surprise me." Maeve extracted a stray pickle from her roast beef sandwich and dropped it onto her plate. "She didn't strike me as someone who made many friends."

"You met her?" asked Jules.

"Briefly." She dipped two fries into a puddle of ketchup and popped them into her mouth. The soggy potato perfection tasted like ten more. "Just before the voice lesson, I had the displeasure of an introduction with the infamous social media star."

"She all but tossed Maeve into the street so we

could get on with the lesson." With fingernails leaving indentations on the cup, Paige plunked down her soda.

"I suppose we don't have to worry about her rudeness anymore." Jules rested her head back on the wooden bench seat. "I don't know about the rest of you, but I'm wiped."

Maeve finished her sandwich in silence. Mulling over the day's events and savoring the expertly blended barbecue sauce, she barely registered the occasional comment made by her dinner companions. A touch of nausea swirled in her stomach. She hadn't consumed this many calories in weeks.

"Looks like we're done here." Finn scanned the few straggling fries on the table. "Paige can wrap up her leftovers. Let's get you ladies back to your cars."

Dislodging herself from the booth, Paige pointed over their heads toward the television hanging behind the bar. "We made the news."

A local newscaster stood in front of The Music Box. The volume wasn't loud enough to hear anything, but she led viewers around the back of the building and gestured toward the yellow police tape cordoning off the parking lot and dumpster. Her actions left little room for interpreting the gist of her story.

"A crime scene is not the kind of press my school needs." Jules's entire face sagged along with her downturned mouth.

With his jaw set, Finn placed a hand on her elbow and led her toward the exit. "Try not to let the reporter bother you. People will talk at first, but this story won't have one iota of impact on the most successful music school in the county."

He was right. So, why did fear fill Mom's eyes?

****

The crisp sheets welcomed Maeve onto the pillowy mattress with a cooling softness against her skin. She lay on her back with eyes closed and allowed the breeze drifting in through the open windows to caress her bare arms and legs. Sighing, she shifted to her side, her mind racing through the events of the day over and over again, refusing to allow sleep to take over. The more sleep eluded her, the more frustrated she grew. After trying in vain to succumb to her exhaustion by switching from one position to another, she gave up and padded into the bathroom to splash water on her face. With any luck, the discomfort of the cold ceramic tiles on her feet and the cool air would help her find solace under the sheets.

Determined to use the same breathing techniques she'd learned in her one and done yoga class, she climbed into bed. Inhaling with the image of Trixie's pink shoes and exhaling with the vision of those bronzed limbs covered in tacky glitter and blood didn't equal a recipe for sweet dreams. Giving up, she flicked the lamp switch and groped for one of the mystery novels on her nightstand. She read the words on the page but failed to comprehend a single line. Only pink pumps, long black hair, and harsh glitter swam before her eyes.

Chapter Three

"Maeve? Are you awake?" Jules's head poked through the slight opening of the bedroom door.

Wasn't it only minutes ago she'd finally found sleep? "No." To her ears, the reply was more of a croak than a word. She burrowed her head under the pillow. A restless night spent tossing and turning would take its toll this morning.

"Well, rise and shine, my dear. We have a guest downstairs."

She snuck a peek at the alarm clock on her nightstand. *Not even eight o'clock yet.* "Tell whoever it is to come back at a more humane hour." Though her eyes were gritty with the sand of exhaustion, she slid her gaze toward the door.

The door creaked all the way open, and Jules marched into the room with her orange tabby cat, Mittens, hot on her heels. She strode toward the windows and yanked open the shades. "Sorry, Sunshine. At the moment, manners are most important." In a flash, she flung open the doors to the walk-in closet and rifled through hangers of clothes. After expelling a series of tsks and mutterings, she selected a few items and tossed them onto the end of the bed. "Here you go. I can stall him for a few minutes with some tea or coffee, but you need to get yourself downstairs pronto."

When the door clicked closed, Maeve counted to ten, then came up for air. Sighing, she sat and swung her legs over the edge of the bed. Resigned to greeting an unwelcome visitor, she picked up the clothes and plodded into the bathroom to change. Whatever Mom chose was better than the ancient, tattered nightgown bought the summer after high school graduation.

Once her face was patted dry, she frowned at her reflection. Rogue, two-toned sprigs stood out all over her head, framing a face so pale someone might believe she hadn't seen a ray of sun since Memorial Day weekend. Only the light freckles smattered over her nose and cheeks added any hint of color to her complexion. A woman with a tad more vanity might attempt to spruce things up with a touch of makeup. The morning after a restless night reliving a murder scene, she wasn't that woman.

Finn would understand her need to return to bed for a few more hours. Untangling the mess on her head and taming the frizz was a futile effort. She yanked fraying strands into a low ponytail and emerged from the bathroom to find a bra and hopefully a baseball cap.

"Maeve!" The muffled voice rang up the stairs through the closed door.

Sometimes, Jules possessed the patience of an infant waiting to be fed. Maeve yanked open the door and hollered. "Let me just throw on a bra! I'll be down in a minute." Spotting a strap peeking out from under the bed, Maeve snapped it up and finished dressing.

As she tramped down the stairs, she cringed at the murmurs of conversation growing louder. The male voice coming from the living room did not belong to Finn. *Great.* Stepping onto the landing and rounding the corner, she found Mom and Detective Taylor seated on the couch with cups of coffee in hand.

"I knew we should have sent her to finishing school."

The snide chirp shot a jolt through her core. "Thanks, Mom. You always did know how to smooth over an embarrassing moment."

In the chilly silence, the detective shifted in his seat.

He'd better brace himself for a few more barbs.

Finally, he cleared his throat. "Good morning, Maeve. I apologize for the early hour and hope you don't mind answering some additional questions." He lifted a mug from the coffee table. "This one's yours."

A small golf ball lodged itself in her throat, but she accepted the coffee. "Thanks." She gripped the handle and sat in one of the mauve wingback chairs opposite him. "I'm pretty sure we covered everything last night at the station. I didn't even know Trixie. Our one introduction didn't last more than ten seconds."

"We've established that fact. Employees and the security cameras at Dog Eared confirmed your whereabouts. Unfortunately, the same can't be said for everyone."

Was air reaching her lungs? Or had she forgotten how to breathe? Either way, her head swam. "You couldn't possibly...I mean, Paige would never..." She struggled to find convincing words in her oxygen-deprived brain.

"I'm here to try and tie up a few loose ends we've come across. What can you tell me about Seamus Wallace?"

Crossing one leg over the other, she hunched

forward and gripped the trembling hand holding her coffee. Detective Taylor's expressionless face watched every move. If circumstances were different, she would have thought him handsome. She'd always been a sucker for black hair and blue eyes. Right now, he turned her insides upside down. *The nerve.* Showing up at her house and accusing one of the sweetest people she'd ever known of homicide. That realization straightened her spine. She lifted her chin and returned his stare. "I've known Seamus since he was in diapers. He wouldn't hurt a fly."

"Are you aware he harbored a secret crush on Trixie?"

She snorted. "I highly doubt it."

"A young man's infatuation with a beautiful woman isn't such an outlandish idea." With eyebrows raised, he sipped the coffee and then placed the mug on the table.

"From what I've heard, her beauty ran skin deep."

"Look, we know Seamus was at The Music Box yesterday. You and Ms. Walsh mentioned seeing him after you returned from the bookstore. We don't know when he arrived, but the security tape showed Paige's arrival, her return, and his departure time. There aren't any cameras in the rear of the building." He leaned forward and clasped his hands. "If he truly arrived after Paige joined you at Dog Eared, that left him with, at a minimum, a solid half hour alone. I want to know if you noticed anything off about him. Was he nervous? Anxious to leave? Disheveled?"

"None of the above. He was happy to see us." The narrowed gaze fixed on her sparked with doubt. Anyone with a shred of common sense knew that breaking eye contact was a sure sign of a guilty conscience. But rather than suffer the scrutinization, she bowed her head and stared into her coffee cup.

"He left a few minutes after you walked in."

Their arrival had taken him by surprise, but he left because he'd finished a job. Prying her gaze from the hypnotizing swirl of liquid in her mug, she glanced up. The detective's probing stare set her heart racing. Despite the pounding in her ears, she spoke with as much conviction as she could muster. "True, but he was not agitated in the least."

"Last night, you relayed a series of events leading to the discovery of the body. What can you tell me about Trixie's relationship with Paige? Would you say they were on friendly terms?"

Jules arched back and blew out a breath.

Friendly? Who could be friends with that icy witch? "They must have gotten along well enough that Trixie was willing to pay her for voice lessons." Though his face remained unreadable, a flicker of suspicion registered in his eyes.

"Paige never mentioned any disagreements between them?" Straightening in his seat, he maintained a deadpan expression, with the exception of an almost imperceptible tilt of his head.

Did inherently disliking someone fall under the umbrella of having a disagreement? Maeve shrunk under his penetrating gaze.

"Look," he said. "From what I understand so far, her online persona aside, Trixie was not what you'd call a warm and fuzzy person. It doesn't sound like she'd made many, if any, friends in Hampton. Given that fact, it wouldn't be out of the realm of possibility for a difference of opinion to crop up now and again."

Yes, but she wasn't about to give him any ammunition to use against her friends. "Paige never mentioned anything."

He lifted his coffee and sipped. "Seamus was allegedly at The Music Box, seeing to technical repairs."

"There's no *allegedly* about it." Jules slapped both palms on her thighs, then leaned forward, jutting stiff, pointed hands into the air. "He was working."

"Did he mention anything about Trixie returning to the school before you and Ms. Walsh arrived?"

"Not a word." He spoke very few words, come to think of it. Was his silence a red flag?

"Let me give you some advice. The vultures are already circling." He stood. "Don't give them anything else to write about."

The room should have remained silent while she figured out what vultures he spoke of. Instead, a droning chatter drifted through the windows. For the first time that morning, she glanced outside. A stream of cars lined the street. The swarm of people wielding cameras and microphones drained the air from her chest. Any hope of finding refuge from the media fanfare surrounding her broken engagement perished with Trixie Bell.

Watching Detective Taylor back out of the driveway and navigate the shouting crowd, Maeve allowed herself to release the breath she'd held for an eternity and faced Jules. "I hope the police aren't limiting their pool of suspects to Paige and Seamus."

Jules tucked a lock of hair behind one ear. "They must be looking into other people. Detective Taylor can't ask for details about suspects you don't know." A small smile touched her lips but failed to reach her eyes. "Everything will sort itself out. Right now, I need to deal with the bazillion voicemails loading my phone and get out a message we're closed today. I can't have music lessons going on while an active crime scene is under investigation outside the back door."

"Can I help with anything?"

"Calista is still asleep upstairs, and Daphne's at The Music Box handling reporters. I need to get over there. Would you mind replying to some messages and handling my business calls? My phone is on the kitchen island with my laptop. Password is still the same for both."

"Sure."

Jules had already grabbed her purse and opened the front door. "You're a love."

Dragging herself upstairs for a quick shower, she noted that nothing slowed Mom down. Sometimes being on the receiving end of that whirlwind of vivacity was draining. So much for coming home to decompress. Of course, Calista chose that moment to emerge from the guest room.

"Maeve-y." Her face broke into a mile-wide, contagious grin. "How long has it been?"

Long, slim arms wrapped her in an embrace. The fruity fragrance of apples tickled her nose. "You smell wonderful." She giggled. "Sorry, weird observation."

"Not at all." Calista released her and stepped back. "I curate my own scents and welcome the compliment. I have thirteen boxes of perfume sitting in my car waiting to sell out at the expo."

Figures. As a child, Calista was obsessed with

plants and flowers. But not in the way little girls enjoy picking daisies. Her penchant for premonitions and insistence on the magical properties of plants unnerved the other children. They didn't know whether to laugh or fear her. So, they avoided her.

The long white hair, snow-white face, and whisper-thin frame reinforced the eerie tales spread about the Cleary witch. As an adult, she'd grown into those striking features and was now hauntingly, but undeniably, beautiful. The fitted black shirt and slim black skirt emphasized her waiflike figure but weren't ideal for a ninety-degree day. "Good luck." Maeve hooked a thumb toward her bedroom. "I should get in the shower."

"Yeah, you never know who else will stop by. I started downstairs earlier but caught an earful of the conversation and hightailed it back to my room." Scrunching up her face, she steepled her fingers under her chin. "How are you doing? This week hasn't shown you any mercy." She jutted one finger into the air. "Wait." After rummaging through an oversized tote, she shoved a tiny glass bottle into Maeve's hand. "Dab a drop on your temples before your nerves take over. Nothing like a hint of lavender to ease anxiety. I have a feeling those journalists outside are a persistent bunch."

"Thanks." A hasty escape was in order before Calista could launch into a dissertation on the healing powers of herbs. "I'll let you get going."

"I do need to run." Turning to leave, she paused, pivoted on one heel, and bit her bottom lip. "See you at dinner?"

Something in her guileless, hopeful expression tugged at Maeve's heart. "Sure." Seeing Calista descend the stairs, she slipped into her room and closed the door. Rolling her neck and shoulders eased only a smidgen of the tension in her muscles. On the plus side, the diversions of a quirky cousin and last night's events prevented dwelling on her broken engagement. Nothing like a murder to distract a woman from her broken heart. Someone should pat her on the back for finding the silver lining in a few days of turmoil.

By the time she'd climbed out of the shower and dressed in a faded purple tank top and white shorts, she couldn't deny her stomach grumbling its discomfort. Thanks to the detective's unsettling interrogation, she'd swallowed little more than a few sips of coffee. The doorbell chiming obliterated her fantasy of visiting the refrigerator. Her chest tightened. For the briefest moment, she ignored the knocking that followed. Maybe the person would give up and leave. But what if Paige stopped by? She jogged downstairs and peered out the stained glass sidelight.

Finn stood on the front porch.

"Oh." She swung open the door and sagged against the frame. "It's you."

"Nice to see you, too. Mind if I come in?" He brandished a cardboard tray holding two coffees in one hand and withdrew a white bag from around his back. "I don't want to find out what happens if a member of your fan club gets hungry."

A roar erupted on the sidewalk.

The restless tingling that coursed through her fingers and toes was an all-too-familiar sensation. The years spent with Greyson failed to numb an ounce of the stage fright she'd suffered since childhood. "Sorry. I didn't mean to be rude. Of course, come in." She stepped aside. "And hey, thanks again for last night."

"Not a problem. Have you eaten breakfast yet?"

"No, and wondering about what's in that bag is just about killing me." She led the way into the kitchen. "Let's sit at the table. This island is a flippin' mess."

The description was an understatement. Mail, magazines, multiple pairs of sunglasses, and myriad paperwork covered every square inch of the island. The eyesore turned Maeve's insides into a twisting ball of stress. She'd never understand how anyone could live day in and day out in such a state of chaos. *Seriously?* How was she supposed to find Mom's business phone in that heap? She'd have to wait for it to ring and then start rooting around.

After retrieving two plates from a cabinet, she sat across from Finn. "Is that vanilla chai I'm smelling?"

"Sure is. I brought you a breakfast feast fit for a champion." From the bag, he extracted an apple turnover and a strawberry-frosted donut.

"My favorites."

"I figured we both deserved a treat this morning."

She broke off a piece of turnover, popped it into her mouth, and let out a sigh. The sugar-and cinnamon-drenched apples were still warm.

His mouth twitched a small smile. "Good?"

She rolled her eyes and broke off another piece. "Better than good. Hey, have you heard from Ryan?"

After swallowing, he shook his head. "No, but I left him a message." Turning his coffee cup in slow circles, he slouched. "I contacted his mom, though. She's freaking out because the longer he's unreachable, the more guilty he looks." He took a sip. "My guess is he just hasn't seen the news yet and is probably wondering why Trixie hasn't called."

"So…" Leaning back, she studied his face. Despite an impassive mask, the twitching muscle along his jawline always revealed any underlying worries. She caught herself wanting to reach for his hand but held back. "You think he's still out of town?"

"Yeah." One of Jules's cats hopped onto his lap and purred with a frenzy. Finn swiped the fluffy tail away from his face and scratched the amorous feline behind the ears. "He told me last weekend he'd be apartment hunting in New York. Trixie recently received a job offer, and they were planning to move." Now the cat was on its back, humming in ecstasy at having its belly stroked. "What's this one's name?"

Maeve peered at the cat. Was this Zu Zu or Belinda? The two calicos were nearly identical. "Not sure. Just keep the fluffball away from me. I haven't taken my allergy meds yet. And stay on topic. What was the job?"

"He wouldn't say." Finn deposited a now-disgruntled Zu Zu or Belinda on the floor. "Supposedly her new employer wanted to personally release the information."

"In the few seconds I spent with her, she didn't strike me as the type to let her fiancé choose their new digs without her input."

He laughed. "You're not wrong. She did all the research and set up the appointments. I'm not sure what kept her in town."

With her turnover decimated and halfway through the donut, Maeve sucked a glob of melting frosting from her finger, sat back, and rested a hand on her stomach. "I totally inhaled my food. If I eat another bite, I'll burst." She pointed at Finn's sparse crumbs. "I see you're still a dainty eater."

A shrill bell rang on the island. Maeve rose and rifled through the mess strewn across the surface until she found the source of the noise. "The Music Box, Maeve speaking." The call already went to voicemail. Oh, well. At least now she knew where the phone was. Gripping the phone, she shrugged and walked to the sliding doors leading to the back deck.

Finn's chair scraped across the tiled floor. "Are you planning to sit?"

"I need to talk to Seamus." The boats bobbing across the ocean resembled white specks.

"Why?" He removed the lid from his cup and sipped. "Hey, does this chai need a little something?" He tore open another sugar packet and dumped the contents into his cup.

No doubt he'd asked the question due more to reflex than interest. Nothing was ever sweet enough for him. "The police were here this morning with more theories. He has a thirty-minute window unaccounted for."

"I don't think he's the type." The wooden seat creaked under his weight.

"Me, either." She grabbed her purse and dropped the phone into the front pocket. "But I'm pretty sure the police visited him today."

"So?" He lifted an eyebrow. "What? You want to harass him next?"

"What if he saw Trixie, or saw something, but was afraid to tell them?"

Both hands jerked up before another word was spoken. "Not your problem."

"But what if I could help?"

He sighed and stood. "I can't imagine how, but I'll come with you. He's living over on Waterfall Terrace now."

Not that Seamus was unfriendly, but the idea of showing up on his doorstep unannounced might seem odd. Finn's company would settle her unease and potentially give the conversation a more casual feel. "Don't you have a coffee house to run?"

"Yeah." He shrugged and gathered the remnants from their breakfast. "I do. But my nieces can manage the place blindfolded without me."

"Phoebe and Myra?" A sharp twinge pierced her chest. "How old are they now?"

"You've been gone longer than you think, and time doesn't stand still. They're both students at UMASS and take turns working shifts during school breaks." After smushing down the trash in the bin, he straightened. His small grin widened as he rocked back on his heels. "You know my sister never had any interest in the business, but her girls love working at the café."

When did Finn's twin nieces become young women? "I have to see them before I leave town."

"They'd love a little reunion. When they were kids, those girls adored you. Remember how they used to call you Auntie Mae Mae?" His eyes crinkled.

"What did they call me after I left?" Some questions are better left unasked. After leaving him high and dry, "Auntie, don't let the door hit you in your blank blank" was the most appropriate term of endearment. She needed to think before she spoke.

He cleared his throat and rubbed the back of his

neck with one hand. "It was a long time ago. I don't remember much other than they stopped mentioning you."

When they'd split up, she lost more than a boyfriend. She lost a family who had become her own. Their high school romance reached an amicable pause during their college years. Bored by small-town life, she chose a school in New York. Though lacking the faintest idea as to what she wanted to study, she refused to be the only one of her friends left behind while everyone else moved on to bigger and better.

Maeve never intended to permanently return to Hampton, but less than a month before her graduation, Dad passed away. She cancelled all job interviews scheduled in the city and headed home the day after receiving her diploma. Uncomfortable deserting her devastated mother, she made a brief detour from her career path and spent three years working full time at The Music Box.

Finn returned from Boston two years into her stay, took over managing Coffee Beans for his mom, and launched a business selling custom blends nationwide.

By the time Jules landed on her feet and adapted to her new normal, Maeve's relationship with Finn was rocketing full speed toward marriage. When she expressed interest in returning to New York, the romance screeched to a halt.

In his opinion, six years of city life was enough. In the best possible way, he was a small-town boy to his core. Happy Beans had been in his family for three generations.

The business passed to him at precisely the same time she dredged up the courage to share the prospect of a job opportunity. A few well-placed connections landed her an interview for an event coordinator position with one of the top events management companies in New York.

Finn apparently loved Hampton Beach more than he loved her. Unwilling to play country mouse to her city mouse, he broke up with her. Before she had time to allow his rejection to sink in, Maeve succumbed to Mom pushing her out the door to pursue long held dreams. Ten years later, and the fact he hadn't made a single contact effort still stung.

He turned on the faucet. "No point standing around here doing nothing." After drying his hands, he tossed the dishtowel on the counter and swung around. Arching one eyebrow, he jerked out a hand with his palm up. "Let's go."

As they strode toward the front door, she nodded and extracted car keys from her purse. "Do you want to take separate cars, so you're not tied to me all day?"

He stepped outside. "Nah, I'm sure you'll have me back before I turn into a pumpkin."

On the heels of sticking her foot in her mouth and overindulging at breakfast, the promise of a drive smothered in awkward silence roiled her nerves more than the hollered demands from photographers stampeding toward the driveway.

Chapter Four

Maeve steered her blue compact car into Seamus's driveway. "After eating that bag of carbs and sugar you called breakfast, we should've walked." Not that the media circus outside Mom's house allowed a leisurely stroll through town.

"You could stand a few extra pounds." Approaching the yellow bungalow, he gave her the once-over.

"I'm well aware, but thanks for making such an astute observation." *Nothing like meeting genuine concern with a snide remark.* Perhaps he deserved an apology. But he could also do with a few lessons on the fine art of timing—starting with when and when not to comment on a woman's appearance. "Stress wreaks havoc on the appetite." On the top step, she jabbed a finger toward the sliver of open space. "People around here have a serious problem tightly closing doors. You'd think he'd be mindful of wasting his A/C." Giving a few light taps, she stepped inside.

"Shouldn't you wait for an invitation?"

At the murmur of voices coming from the back of the house, she put a finger to her lips. "Sounds like he already has company. Seamus, are you home?" After crossing the entryway, she rounded a corner to an open floor plan with a view straight through the living room into the kitchen. Was she hallucinating? No, right in front of the kitchen sink stood Paige and Seamus engaged in a full-on lip-lock. Riveted on the spectacle, she bumped into the sharp corner of an end table. *That'll leave a mark.* A hissing breath slid through her teeth.

The whirring of a wobbling table lamp buzzed.

Paige lurched away from Seamus.

"I-I…" Maeve stepped backward into Finn and stomped on his foot. "We can come back. Sorry for the interruption." She grabbed him by the arm.

"Maeve, wait." Paige jogged around the island and across the living room.

"I just—" She swallowed. "The door was already open, Finn said to wait, but I heard voices and thought—" Paige's hands gripped her shoulders but did little to alleviate a shred of embarrassment. Her face burned.

"Maeve, stop. I intended to tell you about us at some point."

"Is this…" She waggled her fingers between them. "This romance a secret?"

Seamus shot a glance at Paige. "Sort of, but clandestine affairs have a funny way of getting old."

Paige laughed. "So am I." Grinning, she grasped Maeve's hand. "Come on, you have to find the humor here."

"Why is it a secret?" Searching their faces, she found only amusement—not answers. "When did you two get together? Wait, *clandestine*? Does anyone else know?"

Seamus draped an arm across Paige's shoulders. "Our relationship took a turn about six months ago. We haven't gotten around to sharing because your friend here thinks my parents will have a problem with her age."

"And I *know* my parents will give me an earful. They're always bemoaning the fact I haven't found myself a good man yet. But a twenty-six-year-old just starting out won't fit their criteria for the mythical idea of the perfect prospective spouse." She dropped onto the cream sectional. "None of these details matter. We want to be together, and that's that. I wanted some time to enjoy just being a couple before everyone starts giving their well-intentioned, but unwanted, opinions."

Seamus joined her on the couch. "Sit, guys." He gestured toward a nearby loveseat. "And yes, someone does know. Well, knew."

"Knew?" Tucking a throw pillow behind him, Finn sat.

"A few weeks back, we drove out to Westlake Trail and went hiking. The place is massive. I've never once bumped into anyone I know there." He dropped his head and inhaled a deep breath. "But this time around, we hiked right into Trixie's camera lens."

With shaking fingers, Paige adjusted her headband, then gripped his hand. "Yeah, and sweetheart that she was, she refused to cut us out or reshoot her video. The videographer insisted she'd blur us out, but I didn't trust her."

"Who was filming?" asked Finn.

"A friend of hers." Paige tucked both legs under her. "The two of them insisted they filmed at that exact time of the day to capture Trixie in the best light possible." She rolled her eyes. "It was literally the difference of a few minutes. What makes the whole thing even more ridiculous? She was the antithesis of outdoorsy. She wanted to prance around in her cute little hiking outfit and portray herself as a nature enthusiast." With one finger thrust in the air, she threw her head back. "And let me tell you, the next-to-nothing camisole and miniscule shorts didn't exactly imply hiking expertise simply because she paired them with boots."

Seriously. Trixie's wisdom began and ended with cultivating a picture-perfect public image.

Seamus's frown deepened. "Would you mind keeping our relationship to yourselves for the moment? The police have us on their radar because they believe one of us was the last to see her alive. If they find out we're a couple, their wheels might start spinning." He stole a glance at Paige. "Truth is, we were both in The Music Box before Paige met you at Dog Eared. To now say we were together and contradict our original stories placing us at the studio separately would sound fishy. Any time you start changing your story, you appear guilty."

"The camera out front timestamped Trixie's departure and then mine." Paige fidgeted with a loose strand of hair. "Seamus entered through the back door. Only a finite window exists between when the murder could have happened and when we called the police."

Finn nodded and leaned forward, resting tanned forearms on his thighs. "Was anyone else in the back lot?"

"No one," Seamus said.

Maeve directed her gaze toward Paige. Sure, neither of them did a stellar job of keeping in touch recently. But they'd never kept such a bombshell secret from each other. Not in a million years would she have dreamed up this love match. "When I first noticed the door to The Music Box was open, I'm guessing you already knew who was inside?"

"I had a hunch." Paige offered a small smile. "Sorry. Besides, I'd never let you go back to New York without coming clean. I swear."

"Ah, don't apologize." Despite the gravity of the situation, she couldn't stop a small smile from tugging at the corners of her lips. "After all, what's more romantic than a hush-hush affair?"

"So, what brought you here today?" asked Seamus.

"Well, Detective Taylor paid me a visit and asked about you." She paused and allowed a full grin to spread across her face. "I think his assumptions were clearly way off."

"Let me guess." Paige smirked and waggled her fingers above her head. "He said Seamus had a thing for Trixie."

"Yes." Shaking her head, she let out a short breath. "I didn't put much faith in that rumor, but I'd love to hear your side of the story."

"Oh, please," Seamus said. "She was the one blatantly flirting with me. But two things happened. First, I finally told her enough's enough. I was already seeing someone. Second, I called her ma'am during that brief conversation. I think I saw actual steam shoot out her ears." He darted his gaze among his friends. "You're all laughing, but a wound to that woman's ego was no laughing matter. She started telling people I was stalking her. She even posted about her *local stalker* on social media pages."

"Who'd believe her?" asked Finn.

"No one in this town. But the more people brushed

off her stories, the more elaborate they grew."

"Did Ryan buy into it?" Maeve asked Paige.

"I don't know."

Several lines appeared on Seamus's smooth forehead. "The police picked up on the accusations pretty fast and were on my doorstep first thing this morning. I told them I'd stopped by The Music Box yesterday but hadn't laid eyes on her." A timer sounded in the kitchen. "Excuse me for a minute. I have an egg casserole in the oven that'll overcook in seconds."

Seeing the worry etched on Paige's face, Maeve struggled to think of a solution. "She clearly didn't have many friends around here, but can you think of anyone who disliked her enough to hurt her?"

Paige shook her head. "Not really. I think most people made a conscious effort to stay out of her line of fire."

"True." Seamus joined them again. "But I recently installed some system updates at the town hall and overheard her having it out with Vic Adams. They were in his office on the other side of the wall. From what I could tell, the dispute was a real throw down."

"Vic's the town treasurer now," interjected Paige.

"What were they arguing about?" asked Finn.

"I couldn't make out their words through the wall. Only the tone." Seamus straightened. "Oh, and the door slammed on her way out. I'm surprised the thing didn't come off its hinges."

The strain imposed on her friends and the resurgence of media attention filled Maeve with renewed energy. "We need to find out more. The police might want to consider a whole new angle." Out of the corner of her eye, Finn leveled her with a mind-your-own-business look. *Oh, the ride home should be a treat.* She had an end goal in sight, and he knew better than to get in her way. A heavy dose of adrenaline shot through her veins. Vic didn't know it yet, but he had a date with Maeve's pursuit of truth.

****

Ten minutes later, instead of starting the engine, Maeve stared at Seamus's bungalow and allowed the heat inside the car to seep into her bones.

"I can see the cogs inside your head churning away. Still processing the bombshell news of their relationship status?"

"Amongst other things," she said more to herself.

"Can you multitask and get us on the road?" asked Finn.

"Of course." But the stream of questions racing though her mind kept the car parked. She glanced at Finn. "What do you know about Vic? I never knew him well."

"Not much. He's playing a big role in the annual town fundraiser and is on a mission to set a record for donations to his foundation at this year's July Jubilee." He swiped at the sweat beading on his forehead. "You gotta either turn on the A/C or open a window. I'm melting."

"Sorry." She turned the key in the ignition, directed the vents toward Finn, and cranked up the air-conditioner to full blast. "What's the money going toward this year?"

"He wants to completely gut and rebuild the community center. Actually, his plan sounds pretty great. The property will be more like a country club than a community center. I've heard rumors of adding a basketball court, a tennis court, an Olympic-sized pool, and a restaurant of some sort."

"How in the world will he collect enough money?" She shifted into Drive and pulled onto the empty street.

"No idea."

"And what business would Trixie have with him?"

"I don't know." Finn grabbed a container of mints from the console and shook several into his mouth. "But if he had something to do with what happened, you should keep your nose out of it."

Or maybe he should refrain from delivering unsolicited advice. She'd gotten along just fine these last several years without his input. Well, except for getting tangled up with morning television's most hot-to-trot bachelor and hiding out in a vacuum of self-pity for a solid week. Instead of spouting off the series of choice retorts on the tip of her tongue, she swallowed the words and remained quiet until she swung onto her now-empty street and into her driveway. The reporters must have given up waiting on her return. "Thanks for coming with me. I appreciated having someone to share my humiliation with earlier. Barging in on Seamus and Paige took teamwork."

"Any time." After climbing out of the car, he turned and ducked his head inside. "What's next on your agenda?"

"I think I'll head over to The Music Box and see how Mom and Daphne are doing."

"Let me know how it goes."

Once he'd left, she leaned back and closed her eyes. What were the chances he was seeing someone? Better to hit the pause button on that topic. Round three with Finn had all the ingredients of a recipe for disaster.

****

The media activity outside the music school forced Maeve to park several blocks away. By the time she'd trekked over and snuck in the back entrance, she was a hot mess. Sweat dripped down her face. No doubt her shirt had pit stains. Humidity never failed to turn her ponytail into a dollop of cotton candy sprouting from the back of her head.

Jules took one look at her daughter and recoiled two steps. "You, my dear, are a complete fright. Go freshen up in the powder room, and then Daphne and I can fill you in on the goings-on around here today."

Daphne emerged from the voice room. "Maeve. Get over here you gorgeous thing, and give me a hug."

At the sight of Daphne's enormous stomach, Maeve stiffened, a strangled gasp seizing her throat. Swatting away tears, she rushed forward with arms open. "Look at you, beautiful. You're positively glowing." Daphne's size made it impossible to wrap two arms around her.

She drew back laughing with one hand on her stomach and the other sweeping stray, spiral curls of chestnut hair out of her eyes. "Sorry. These guys make it hard to do just about anything and everything these days."

"These guys?" Maeve asked. "Are we talking twins?" She narrowed her gaze at Jules. "No one told me two little Daphnes were on the way."

"Of course, I did."

Leave it to Mom to pull a face with the same disdain reserved for teenagers.

"You simply don't listen to half of what I say."

Maeve returned the scowl, but the excitement

coursing through her veins refused to allow anything to dampen her mood. "When are you due? What are you having?" She gestured toward Daphne's burgeoning bump.

"When you said two Daphnes, you were correct. They're both girls. As to when I'm due?" She shrugged and grinned. "Just about any second."

"Why are you still here?" Another accusatory glance hurtled toward Jules. Seeing her put up her hands in defense did little to appease Maeve.

"Don't look at me," said Mom.

"She's right." Daphne shrugged. "I go crazy sitting at home. I had everything ready in the nursery months ago. Now I pace around, watching the minutes tick by and waiting for my water to break. At least here, I have distractions. The bigger problem? Your mom still hasn't found my replacement."

"You're irreplaceable." Though she'd dipped her head toward a sheet of music, the downturn of Jules's mouth was unmistakable.

At the sincerity in Mom's voice, a bit of the stiffness in Maeve's shoulders released. "She is, but you need to figure something out."

"Maybe you could stick around a few months instead of a few weeks, and help out your dear old mother."

Although spoken in jest, the comment struck a nerve. *No one else is banging down the door with a better offer.* "It wouldn't be out of the question."

"Oh, Maeve, I was joking. I know you have a career and a life to get back to." Sifting through the heap of paper on her desk, Mom dragged a finger down several pages.

Time to reveal the rest of her sob story. "At the moment, I don't."

Jules yanked off her reading glasses and jerked up her head. "What are you talking about?"

Maeve darted a glance at Daphne, who'd always been one of her favorite people, despite the fact the woman was compelled to share local gossip as if it were her life's work. Half the town would hear Maeve's tale of woe before the day was out. "I don't have anything to return to. No fiancé, no job, not even a place to live. When—if—I go back, I'll need to hunt for an apartment. And that search should be super easy, considering my income is currently zero dollars per week."

For a few deafening moments of silence, Jules gaped. "When did you leave your job?"

On the verge of sagging to the floor, Maeve dragged the nearest wooden chair to the desk. "I resigned about three months ago. I'd been unhappy for a while. Those people, Mom." She tilted back her head and searched the ceiling, wishing the proper adjectives dangled from above. "I'd book these amazing events. But instead of thanking me and handing over the reins, clients started right in with their prima donna demands that were often completely unreasonable, not to mention impossible."

"So, you just quit? With nothing else in the pipeline?"

The waves of horror screwing up Mom's pretty features made it difficult to continue. The mounds of paperwork scattered about her kitchen, car, and desk implied Jules was a walking tornado in heels. In truth, she was the crowned goddess of organized chaos and a planner to the core of her soul. She ran on two speeds. First, set a goal. Second, succeed. Maeve cleared her throat and forced her thickening tongue to work. "Greyson and I were already engaged, and I'd given up my apartment to move in with him. He suggested I quit and take some time to figure out my next move." Lowering her gaze, she gave a slow shake of the head and took a breath. "I jumped on the idea."

How to explain the overwhelming anxiety she'd experienced working at a company whose expectations for perfection exceeded all dimensions of reality? In a business dependent on external vendors managing their own scheduling delays and inventory hiccups, she existed in a soul depleting limbo of dread. Jules had no frame of reference for such things. If she'd ever experienced the fear of failure, and that's a strong *if*, the emotion only served as additional motivation to triumph.

For a moment, Jules bowed her head, covering her mouth with a fist. "So, you planned to depend on him while you, what, found your true calling?" With a slap, she flattened her palm on the desk.

Maeve cast a sideways glance at Daphne. Would it be too much to ask for a bit of help from the audience?

"No one could fault you. Sounds like that job took a toll on your health." Daphne skimmed her gaze up and down. "Looks like it, too. Don't get me wrong; you're still pretty as a picture, but you could do with a bit more meat on your bones. And I know you. When you're under stress, the appetite's always the first to go."

True facts. Quitting her job upped the ante. Surrounded by friends whose sole focus was on who had what and who had more, she lagged behind in a constant race she could never win. Embarrassed to say anything to Greyson, she spent the bulk of her savings and maxed out her credit cards to keep up with his lavish lifestyle. But at least she didn't have to worry about living expenses.

The demise of the relationship sent her into a financial free fall. Now she ran on empty and scraped out coffee change from the bottom of her purse to minimize doing further damage to her credit card balance.

"Why haven't you said anything until now?"

Jules's snapping tone hurled her into the present. "I was embarrassed." She tilted her head. "Come on, Mom. You know you're a hard act to follow. Never once in your life would you have allowed yourself to become dependent on anyone."

"Well, you went down that road." She shoved her glasses onto her head as a makeshift headband and gave a dismissive wave. "You can see for yourself how things turned out."

Stung, Maeve blinked back the tears threatening to spill. Poor Daphne stumbled into the awkward, front row seat of a mother-daughter sparring match. "Yup. Lesson learned."

Jules's owl-eyed expression softened. "If you had the luxury of finding your passion, I'd never expect you to stay in a job you loathed." She clasped her hands together. "Well, that settles it. You're hired. Daphne can fill you in on everything over the next few days so you're ready to take over after those babies make their debut."

"Absolutely," Daphne said. "You have no idea how

relieved I am to have someone to pass the torch to. I had visions of traipsing over here every day with two infants in tow."

A few of the enormous weights on her shoulders lifted. She could always count on Jules to put her through an emotional wringer. But in her defense, every time that inflated motherly confidence suffered another blow, the woman experienced genuine physical pain. Those big dreams came from a place of love. "Thank you, Mom. And Daphne, full disclosure, thank you in advance because you have your work cut out in training me." She stood and arched her back. "If you'll both excuse me, I'll take my mother's sage advice and go clean myself up."

On her way to the restroom, she squeezed Daphne's arm and winked. Flicking on the light and closing the door behind her, she winced at the fright Mom spoke of staring back through the mirror. With limited resources at her disposal, she resorted to splashing cold water on her face and under her armpits. Using more water, she raked her frizzing hair into the tightest bun she could manage without a comb or brush handy.

Although the image reflected in the mirror had somewhat improved, a shower and a change of clothes beckoned. Devoid of the vanity gene, she emerged from the restroom to raised voices emanating from the studio.

All five feet of Jules, with hands on hips, shouted at Detective Taylor.

Great. Despite best efforts, Maeve still smelled like a goat. The idea of another grilling set off a roaring round of heart palpitations.

Chapter Five

On featherlight steps, Maeve tiptoed behind The Music Box's front desk. Better to draw as little attention to herself as possible.

Detective Taylor stood just inside the entrance.

"You call yourself a police officer? You have eyes, don't you?" Flailing her arms, Jules gestured toward Daphne. "For the love of all nonsense, look at her. The last thing a woman in her condition needs is a police interrogation. On what planet is this hogwash considered acceptable behavior?"

If the crinkles around his eyes were any indication, he was slightly amused at Jules's mother bear level of protective instinct for Daphne. How long until amusement veered toward annoyance? How to diffuse Mom's wrath? "Let's try to remain calm. I'm sure the detective isn't here to harass Daphne."

"Mrs. Cleary, I assure you, an interrogation isn't on the agenda," he responded. "I promise I'm only here to ask a few questions. Daphne Garrett works for you and might have seen something suspicious."

"Jules, don't worry." Daphne patted her boss's arm. "He's not here to badger me."

"Not in the least." He removed a small notepad and a pen from his back pocket.

"Fine. You can sit at my desk." Jules took Daphne's elbow and glared at Detective Taylor. "I don't like to see you spending too much time on your feet." Several lines etched across her forehead.

Striding to the back of the studio, Detective Taylor caught Maeve's eye and mouthed *thank you*.

Although she responded with a curt nod, he was no friend of hers. His intrusion surpassed the definition of unwelcome. She only intervened to help Daphne appear cooperative. Saving him a dose of irritation wasn't on her priority list.

After nearly ten minutes of discussion met with snorts, sighs, and glares from Jules, Detective Taylor scanned his notepad, jotted a final thought, and stood. "Thank you for your time."

"I'll walk you out," Maeve said. "But don't expect to chitchat on the sidewalk. Those vultures you mentioned this morning are out for blood." The weight of Mom's and Daphne's unwavering stares hastened her pace. "Get everything you need?"

"Yeah, I already knew Daphne had a solid alibi. Her obstetrician's office confirmed an appointment during the small window of time the crime took place. I wanted to know if she'd noticed anything unusual in the last few weeks, either in the area or with Trixie's behavior."

A fraction of the thorns pricking her insides subsided. He did have a job to do and a case to solve. "Sorry about my mom. Daphne is like a surrogate daughter. She started piano lessons here at six years old and never left." Was a smile fighting to break through? The twitching corners of his mouth slid into a full grin and revealed the most charming pair of unexpected dimples. She bit back the urge to advise him to smile more often and instead relished the satisfaction of cracking his stony face. Maybe he was human, after all. Not for the first time, she noted he was a quite nice-looking human, as well. Another opportunity to take advantage of this rare good mood might not present itself. "Do you have anyone else on your list of suspects other than Paige and Seamus?" A figment of her imagination, the smile vanished.

"I'm not at liberty to discuss an active investigation."

"Of course. And I don't want to point the finger at anyone, but I'm certain Trixie didn't get along with several people. In fact, someone overheard her having it out with Vic Adams just last week."

His face remained frozen except for his eyes widening for a millisecond. "Who?"

Naming Seamus as her source would resonate as nothing more than finger-pointing. "I think a town hall employee shouldn't be ruled out."

"You think?" He waited.

The longer she remained tightlipped, the more his gaze narrowed. Her stomach flipped over. Now she'd put herself on his radar as someone reluctant to share information. How fair was that theory when all she wanted to do was point him toward a probable suspect?

"Do you have any specifics on what was said?"

Did the man know how to blink? Who holds eye contact for that long? Well, someone who didn't want to miss the slightest twitch, flinch, or other hint of guilt. She tossed a casual shrug but was sure the movement resembled more of a strained lurch. "I wish." Their conversation officially hit a wall of concrete.

"Well, let me know if you hear anything else."

"I will," she agreed. "Have a nice afternoon." Once

inside the frigid air-conditioned room, she sagged against the door, inhaled a long breath through her nostrils, and exhaled a slow hiss through her mouth.

The clacking of the keyboard drowned out the country music Jules played when the school was empty. Daphne typed what sounded like a million words per minute.

Jules marched toward her. "Maeve, has anyone called today?"

Had the phone rung since this morning's missed call? She shuffled around in her bag for Mom's bedazzled, cat face case and withdrew the cell. Despite several stabs at the power button, the screen remained black. "Sorry, the battery died."

"Great. Two thousand messages are probably waiting." She sighed. "Let's call it a day, ladies. We'll remain closed tomorrow. If you get an early enough start, Daphne'll transfer a good amount of knowledge to you." She took the phone and grabbed her purse and keys. "How's nine for you, Daph?"

"Perfect."

"Nine, it is." After flashing Daphne a quick grin, Maeve faced Jules. "Mom, can you give me a lift? My car's parked by Tess's Tresses."

"You traipsed all the way here from Tess's in this heat?" She threw her head back. "No wonder you looked like you just crossed a desert. I was afraid you were trying out that beachy wave hairdo everyone's going for. That look is more of a hair *don't* in my book." She opened the door and groaned. "Heavens to boilin' Betsy! The air's as thick as pea soup out there. I hope this heat wave breaks soon."

On her way out, Maeve stopped at the desk for a

sticky note and snatched a pen bearing The Music Box piano key logo. An old-fashioned to-do list for the following day was in order.

So much for escaping sight unseen out the back door. Several reporters waited and dove into action vying for attention and a comment. Even if she cared to waste time deciphering who asked what, she was rendered unable to form a response by the deafening commotion. However, a few key phrases stood out. More than once, someone hollered "Trixie and Seamus," "Where's Ryan?," and "love triangle." Desperate to know what story the media led with, she hopped inside the car and searched for the local online paper on her phone. Trixie took up prime real estate as the main story on the homepage written by none other than Finn Keaton. She blinked twice to ensure she hadn't misread the byline. "Finn is still writing?" She didn't intend to speak aloud.

"He's been writing for *The Hampton Post* for years." Mom kept her gaze on the road but shot Maeve a quick glance. "Just short pieces."

Mom was right. The article was three paragraphs long and included the few details she already knew about the case. Thank goodness he'd stayed true to the facts. If the press at the music school was any indication, the media was abuzz with the possibilities of Paige, Seamus, or Ryan murdering Trixie out of jealousy. Love triangle? If they only knew.

She exited out of the article and stuck a sticky note to the back of her phone as a makeshift hard writing surface while pondering the fact Finn hadn't given up writing altogether. This news added a fleeting glimmer of joy to an otherwise draining morning.

Junior year of high school, she'd joined the school newspaper for the sole purpose of having a reason to spend time with him. Her job was to report on school events and the final scores of various games. Her heart was never in it, but she remembered how dedicated he'd been to churning out articles more befitting a national news outlet.

His long hours spent writing and editing paid off in the form of an acceptance letter to Boston College the following year.

By then, they'd become the poster children for high school sweethearts. What would have happened if she'd asked him to stay?

He received acceptance letters to several excellent schools in New York. But none offered a comparable program.

Even though bits of her heart shattered into tinier pieces each day of their last summer together, she encouraged his dream. She'd envied Finn for having a clear goal and following his path. At eighteen, she didn't have the foggiest clue as to what she wanted to do with her life. All of her friends applied to college. To avoid being left behind, she did the same and set her sights on The Big Apple.

At the end of August, Finn left for Boston.

She headed to New York in pursuit of a bachelor's degree in "what do I want to be when I grow up." Although still lacking an answer four years later, she'd made many friends, developed a love for party planning, and graduated with a degree in hospitality and tourism management.

Funny how Finn's detail-oriented life planning and her fly-by-the-seat-of-her-pants lifestyle landed them both back in Hampton. Finn made it clear a long time ago he was here to stay. Was she?

Against her better judgment, she typed in an online search for more stories on Trixie. One scan of the list of articles filled her mouth with the bitter taste of bile. As expected, a slew of titles mentioned The Music Box. But many also implicated Greyson Walker's jilted fiancée as an accessory to old friend, and equally dejected, Paige Walsh's crime of passion.

Journalists ran full speed ahead with the theory Paige killed Trixie, and Maeve helped cover up the murder.

No wonder another media storm kicked off fiercer than the one surrounding her breakup. Sure, public interest in Trixie's death existed. But the potential involvement of a celebrity's ex spiraled mere curiosity and concern into a fever-pitched mania. A mind-numbing chill replaced the symptoms she usually associated with anxiety. Did she have a hope in holy Toledo of salvaging her reputation? And what impact would the accusations have on Mom's business?

****

An impromptu, late afternoon visit from Ida and Luanne upended the fragile hint of calm Maeve managed to cultivate. The mug of hot tea, the softest chenille throw Jules owned, and the most mindless television show she could find provided little protection from their excited chatter. So much for tucking into another soothing episode of *Homely Homes*. After turning off the TV, Maeve sighed and dropped the remote onto the adjacent cushion.

They pranced in, all in a fluster.

"Please, would someone tell me why this woman is

wrapped in a blanket during a heat wave?" shrieked Luanne.

"Tell your friend to ease up on the arctic temps she maintains in this house, and we'll talk." Another sore spot between her and Jules. Those beloved cats and their fur coats came first.

"You two can hash out your utilities later. We have news. The police are searching for Ryan." Perching on the corner of the couch, Luanne lifted a hand to her throat and leaned toward Maeve. "You know Ryan's mom works in our real estate office. Well, would you believe the police stopped by this morning and asked if she knew his whereabouts? Poor Delores nearly fell to pieces."

At the blast of garlic wafting into her face, Maeve lifted a hand to her nose and gave a slight cough. Why couldn't Mom keep mints in the candy dish instead of chocolate?

"I do feel for the woman," interjected Ida. "But the nerve of her to imply he's also a potential victim is almost too much. I never did trust that boy." She puffed out her slender chest, sat on the edge of a wingback chair, and smoothed the many layers of her top.

She'd replaced her usual morning athleisure with cropped navy pants and a white blouse with more ruffles than anyone should ever be allowed to wear.

"Even as a child, he was sneaky." Ida curved her lips into a sneer. "Did you know one time I caught him creeping around Jules's desk at The Music Box? I just know he was planning on stealing something."

Jules shook her head. "I remember that day. He wanted to leave a sweet note for Paige. Those two were quite the item back then."

Bright red fingertips flicked the air. Ida rolled her eyes. "I didn't buy that easy alibi for two seconds."

Luanne's head bobbled around on her neck as if the harder she nodded, the more validity was given to the accusatory statements. She routinely deferred to Ida's opinion, and today was no exception. "I knew him well, and he was not a thief." Uncoiling her legs, Maeve planted both feet on the floor and stiffened. How dare they drag his name through the mud?

"Don't be so naïve, Maeve. When a healthy young woman turns up dead, police *always* suspect the husband or boyfriend first. Everyone knows *that*." Ida's sweet drawl failed to conceal her underlying condescension.

Again, Luanne's puppet head bobbed up and down. Shimmering highlights dusted across her shoulders.

Did these two women have nothing better to do with their time? At the risk of sounding defensive, she had only one strategy to shift the focus off Ryan. "I've heard whispers something was going on between Vic Adams and Trixie." As the words tumbled out, Maeve flinched at the sliver of regret sliding down her spine. She was reluctant to point a finger at someone innocent, but plenty of players were entering this game.

"Not romantically, surely?" gasped Luanne.

The three women fixed their gazes on her with laser-beam intensity. *Mission accomplished.* Maybe they'd have something to offer. "Oh, no." Tapping her chin with an index finger, she paused for dramatic effect. "At least, I don't think so."

"Well, spit it out, Maeve." Widening her gaze, Mom fidgeted with the string of pearls around her neck.

"You must know about their big blowout in his

office."

Ida snorted. "Please. That tiff was merely a little spat about the fundraiser. Nothing to do with romance, or *murder*, for that matter."

Now to spring the trap. "You're always on top of everything in Hampton. I knew you'd have heard."

"Heard *about* it?" Pitching forward, Ida slapped both hands on her knees. "I was at the town hall that day picking up the plot plan for a property and got a firsthand earful of the whole to-do. The door to his office was closed, so the voices were muffled. But I could tell they were squabbling over money because Trixie said, more than once, something about getting paid. My guess is she wanted payment for an appearance at the July Jubilee." She guffawed and threw up her hands. "Imagine having the nerve to ask for a fee while everyone else is making donations to help a good cause? I don't like to speak ill of the dead, but that woman did nothing other than take, take, take."

Digesting the information, Maeve furrowed a brow. "Why in the world would she expect him to pay her?"

"I'm not even going to try to answer that question. All I know is she used to strut around with her hand perpetually stretched out, waiting for people to drop money into her palm. She held the lofty impression that gracing people with her presence was worth a pretty penny. Just ask Tess." She held up a hand and ticked off three fingers. "Trixie stiffed her for a two-hour visit that entailed a cut, color, and blowout under the misassumption Tess would feel honored to have her sit in a beauty salon chair and post a positive review."

Luanne inched to the edge of her seat, fixed her

posture, and added a few more head bobs. "And remember when Priscilla spent a month altering a cocktail dress to ridiculously detailed specifications? But when Trixie went to pick up the final product, do you think she produced a credit card? No, she did not." Droplets of spittle flew. "Trixie said she did Priscilla the favor because 'didn't she know everyone wants to dress Trixie Bell?' " She puffed up at the pompous assumption. "Priscilla's no doormat. She kept the dress and told her to come back with the money due."

A million questions flashed through Maeve's mind, but she forced herself to swallow them, rather than risk an end to the flood of information. She jerked her head toward Luanne's buzzing phone and prayed Ida would continue. "I'm willing to bet you have many similar stories to share."

"And then some." Pursing her lips, Ida crossed her legs. "I distinctly remember Trixie saying Vic owed her. Some words were harder than others to make out. But she said, at least twice, he *owed* her." She stretched out the word, making a large *O* with her lips. "I also remember her threatening to tell everyone. Tell everyone what? Well, your guess is as good as mine." She glanced sideways at Luanne. "Luanne thinks I misunderstood that part because she doesn't believe Trixie wanted everyone to know her participation came with a price tag instead of a donation."

Overcome with a restless urge to move, Maeve stood. How to graciously excuse herself? A blur of scrambled excuses rattled around in her brain. She gave up and grabbed her phone from the coffee table. "Look at that. I've enjoyed chatting with you ladies so much, I didn't realize the time." She edged around the table and planted a peck on each of their cheeks. "I have to get going." Hopefully, the exaggerated squinting of her eyes and scrunched-up forehead conveyed sincere disappointment. "Mom, I'll be home by six." She flung her purse over one shoulder and blew an air kiss. The best way to obliterate any chance for inquiries was to get out of the house.

She bounded down the porch stairs, hopped into her car, shifted into Drive, and drove to the end of the street. No one with a pulse hammering out of her chest should operate a vehicle. She pulled to the curb, put the car in Park, and took a moment to catch her breath. Based on Ida's and Luanne's observations, the odds of Vic's involvement with the murder were increasing.

Luanne was right. If Vic paid Trixie for an appearance at the Jubilee, she'd want the arrangement kept under wraps. She was threatening to tell everyone something else. Something Vic needed her to keep quiet. One location in town might provide a few answers.

Chapter Six

The time was almost four thirty. Town hall offices closed to the public at five. Maeve would go in, hide, wait, and then find a way to sneak out. A galloping heart rate pummeled her chest. If she allowed herself to think about what might happen, she'd never put the plan in motion.

A dizzying wave of vertigo glued her to the seat, but she forced herself out of the car and followed the sidewalk to the main entrance. The white staircase which usually welcomed residents with open arms now loomed before her as an imposing reminder she was on the verge of becoming a full-fledged trespasser. But she'd made it this far. With a thundering roar in her ears, she jogged up the steps, into the building, and ducked into the nearest restroom to wait out the last few minutes until closing.

Bad idea. Chances were good someone might stop in before leaving. She pressed her back against the door, squeezed her eyes shut, and prayed to pull off an award-winning performance, if the need arose. She'd pretend to be on her way out. No one would think twice about a woman exiting the ladies' room. But if her current state of trembling from head to toe was any indication, *this* woman would be lucky to place one foot in front of the other without collapsing.

****

The town hall might close at five, but few employees were in a rush to get home. A never-ending drone of voices from the hallway carried into the restroom. Maeve texted Jules a vague line about running late and proceeded to hide in a stall for over an hour. The risk was minimized but not non-existent. Her frayed nerves couldn't handle one more minute of waiting. Time to either hit the road or follow through with her plan, flimsy as it was.

She poked her head into the hallway and found it empty. *Finally*. Tiptoeing toward the treasurer's office, Maeve held her breath. Why, why, why did she think this was a good idea? She had no business skulking around this building. Surely, someone would recognize her. And then what? She'd have to concoct a plausible reason for her visit. The opportunity to plan each step of this escapade passed long before stepping one foot inside. Time was of the essence.

As she approached the housing authority office, Maeve strained to decipher the muffled words sounding behind the door. When the conversation paused, she bolted into a nearby men's room. Two feet shuffled inside one of the stalls. She dashed into the only other one available. Locking the door, she glanced down at her shoes. The tiny space allowed enough room to straddle the seat and flatten her body against the wall. Wedge sandals eliminated the option of standing on the toilet. If only she'd had a chance to change or think of these things before leaving home.

The man exited the adjacent stall.

Through the crack stood none other than Vic Adams. With any luck, he'd head home after this pit stop. Invoking the patience of a saint, she waited a few minutes before creaking open the door to the hallway. The housing authority's door was closed. She crept along the carpeted path to the treasurer's office and peered through the window. The room was dark and empty. *Now what?* This afternoon's conversation with the clucking hens of Clover Lane served as the catalyst for this excursion but left little time to ponder what might go wrong. She twisted the doorknob. It didn't budge.

A whistling man swung a cleaning cart around the corner.

Her mouth went dry. Swallowing was a challenge. Talking might prove impossible.

"Good evening." He smiled and unlocked the office next door.

Upon closer inspection, he was in his early twenties. Brown hair due for a cut at least three months ago brushed his cheekbones. Choking on a hello, she covered her mouth and coughed. "Um, I'm a bit embarrassed." She slid her hand to her strangling throat. "I had a meeting with Mr. Adams earlier, and would you believe I left my keys inside?"

The man sized her up. "Can you be quick? I'm vacuuming that office next."

He must have concluded she posed little threat. "You are a lifesaver." She gave him the sweetest smile she could muster up.

Better to leave the lights off and avoid the chance of anyone catching her snooping. A cursory glance around told her she'd never have enough time to do a thorough search. Not that she knew what she was searching for, so maybe it didn't matter. She'd start with the desk. In the movies, incriminating evidence always turned up in secret desk compartments.

After coming up empty-handed, she cursed the movies for giving her a false sense of hope. A jacket hung on a wall hook. Maybe she'd find something in one of the pockets. As she dashed across the room, one of her impractical shoes caught, and she toppled to her knees. In her haste, she hadn't noticed the cord running from the wall to the desk.

Her hair fell across her face, and she fumbled around for the now missing shoe. When her hand landed on the heel, she slouched with a short exhale, sat back to place it on her foot, and massaged both throbbing knees. Her eyes finally adjusted to the dark. That fact, in combination with the light peeking through the window shades, revealed several items had fallen out of her purse. Across the floor lay her phone, with something leaning on it.

Resolving to purchase pocketbooks that zipped closed in the future, she stuffed everything back inside her open bag and crawled forward. With one arm extended, she lifted the piece of baseboard from her phone. She'd just slide the wood into place and be on her way.

On closer examination, stacks of something stood inside the wall. *Money! Bundles of money!* She lurched back. The rattle of a cart's wheels approaching froze her in place. As the doorknob turned, she shoved the baseboard into the wall, grabbed her phone, and jangled her keys.

Mr. Helpful switched on the light. "You're still here?"

She flipped the errant hair out of her eyes. "Sorry. I found my keys but tripped in the dark." To her ears, the laugh she choked out sounded more maniacal than cutesy. "Then it took some time to find them."

"Are you okay?"

"Yeah, fine." She stood and tugged down the tee which had ridden up during her crawl across the floor. "Thanks again." The bored expression and reflexive "have a good night" drowned out by the vacuum turning on told her she was in the clear.

Not daring to run, she rushed out of the office and toward the exit. Once outside and on the front stairs, a welcome chill caressed her bare arms. Today's warm temperatures dropped over the last few hours. She closed her eyes, inhaled the sweet scent of chocolate emanating from a nearby fudge shop mingled with the fresh air, and willed her pulse to return to its normal rhythm. Fluttering open her heavy lids, she groaned out loud. Relief morphed into dread.

"Miss Cleary, a little late for town hall business, no?" A half smile curved Detective Taylor's lips.

She glanced at the building and then at the detective, moving her mouth in a vain effort to form words. Every nerve ending in her body rang with intensity until each one snapped. "I didn't notice the time."

"Something wrong?" He raised an eyebrow.

"Not at all."

"The building is closed. Mind if I ask who your business was with?"

The slight frown darkening his face proved he knew she couldn't answer that request.

"You do understand this little thing called trespassing is a crime?" The same eyebrow twitched up again as he hooked thumbs through his belt loops.

"I was stuck in the bathroom." Despite the heat flaming her cheeks, those words provided a perfect excuse. "I think I'm coming down with something." *Talk about hitting a new low.* Was that skepticism or amusement reflecting in his eyes?

A group of teenagers passed between them, most likely on their way to the adolescent hot spot, Pizzarama, at the end of the street. Maeve followed the crowd's progress, then slid her gaze to Detective Taylor's deadpan expression.

"I suppose someone might buy that story. Are you feeling better?"

"When I know you've given up pinning a murder on innocent people, I'll feel better." Sounding like a sulky five-year-old was, at best, unattractive.

"My investigation isn't personal." He shrugged and planted his feet shoulder width apart. "My job is to follow the facts."

"In there"—she waved a hand behind her—"I found proof. Well, possible proof." *Oh, to wipe the grin threatening to emerge on his face.*

"Before or after your trip to the restroom?"

She tucked locks of hair behind both ears, folded her arms across her chest, and clenched her teeth. He wasn't the only one who could strike a pose.

"Why are you looking for proof?" He cocked his head to one side and smirked. "Were you recently hired by the Hampton Police Department, and I didn't catch the news bulletin?"

Sarcasm ranked low on her favorite forms of humor, and his snarky tone was most definitely absent from her catalogue of laughable tactics. To him, she probably looked more like a kindergartener pouting than the intended self-assured woman. "I just happened to accidentally stay past closing and found something unusual."

"I've got to get back to the station." Stepping aside, he swept one hand toward her car. "Would you care to meet me over there, and tell me all about it?"

The threat of another round of questioning at the station set off an explosive batch of butterflies. Would he pursue the trespassing thing? "Sure." Twenty minutes later, she sat across from Detective Taylor and relayed the whole story, starting with several witnesses who overheard Vic's argument with Trixie and some of the choice phrases plucked from the noise. The big finale entailed her discovery of the stacks of cash hidden in the wall of Vic's office. Throughout her spiel, Detective Taylor's face remained expressionless.

After a moment of silence, he clasped his hands and perched them under his chin. "You've crafted an intriguing tale, Maeve. I can't say any of the information proves Mr. Adams was involved in Trixie's murder. If he's stealing money, we're talking about a very different crime. For all we know, he's a chronic gambler hiding the money from his wife."

A steam of frustration nearly propelled her off the seat. "I know. But what if Trixie discovered the stash and threatened to tell everyone? Maybe she said he owed her something in return for staying quiet."

He nodded. "The hidden money's an angle and might be helpful. But I'd prefer you let us do our jobs while you do whatever it is you do. Trespassing is illegal. Anyone else inside could've just as easily seen you tonight, and our conversation wouldn't revolve around your suspicions about Vic." As he rose, his chair scraped across the floor in a clear dismissal. "Have a good night."

"That's it?" She didn't bother to stifle the edge creeping into her voice.

"Maeve, I can take statements. I can't share information."

She sighed, sat back, and roved her gaze across his desk. "Is that Trixie's file?"

He lifted the manila folder and gave it a light shake. "This paperwork is none of your business." He stood the folder upright and tapped it on his desk. "Thank you for your time. And do me a favor: try to restrain yourself from investigating on your own. Let me know if anything comes up, and we'll handle it here. You have my card."

"I do." She was as done with him as he was with her. Not that she blamed him for extracting details rather than reporting leads. But while a deepening shadow of suspicion loomed over her and her friends, thanks to the ever-growing list of accusations spun in a media web of sensational stories, watching and wondering from the sidelines wasn't an option. Vic might worry about the police setting their sights on him, but he'd never imagine Maeve had reason to accuse him of any wrongdoing. Now to find a way to use that misplaced assumption to her advantage.

****

As Maeve stepped out of the car, she breathed in a cloud of barbecue heaven tingeing the salty air. Much like everything else in her life, Jules excelled at cooking. Even the prospect of an evening with Calista loomed brighter if a Swiss and caramelized onion burger was on the menu. Instead of going inside, she followed a faint beat of music along the flagstone walkway and through the wrought iron gate leading to the back of the house.

On the deck, Jules danced, waving a set of tongs in one hand and a metal spatula in the other.

At the same time, Calista swayed along with eyes closed and a martini glass held high. "Thought you'd never get here, Maeve-y." Calista's eyes remained closed.

Creepy Calista hadn't lost her touch. Without cracking so much as an eyelash-size peek, she had a knack for knowing when someone arrived, even if they had yet to be seen, heard, or announced. This talent was one of the many mystical skills that spooked Maeve and her friends as children.

In an instant, Jules stopped. "Where have you been? We sailed past famished hours ago but didn't want to eat without you. Another few minutes, and I might have collapsed."

"Sorry." Maeve climbed the stairs. Tendrils of guilt flickered in her chest. "I should've called." Seeing Calista glide forward, Maeve shrunk back from the narrowed gaze.

"You look like you've had a night." Calista snaked an arm around her waist and steered her toward the small bar. "Let's get you something to take the edge off."

Seconds later, a glass of chilled white wine sat on the counter.

"Sip, then spill." With hands clasped together, Calista draped her torso across the bar.

Sip was the key word. The cool fruity liquid slid down her throat...perfect for a warm night. Dinner outside with a background symphony of ocean waves might heal her frazzled state. But a burger was in order if she intended to stay awake for more than an hour. "I don't want to drop my tale of misery on you. Tell me about the expo."

Calista wiggled long, white-painted nails toward her. "I came. I saw. I sold. End of story. Your turn."

"Congratulations. I'm glad you made some sales." She could ignore the no-nonsense look on Calista's face and call it a night. But to put voice to today's events might help her figure out what she was missing. She took another fortifying sip and set down the glass with a soft clink. "I would've been here hours ago, but I got caught trespassing and was hauled into Hampton PD."

"You what?" For a moment, Jules stood frozen except for her mouth opening and closing without uttering a word. Finally, she expelled a blast of air from her lungs, left the burgers to char, and marched toward Maeve.

"A minor detour. Not a big deal." Maeve hunched over the bar and swirled the contents in her glass. Mom would turn the whole fiasco into a *major* deal.

"Trespassing is a felony." A plume of smoke bloomed behind Jules.

"Mom, do you want me to take over?" Stiffening, she sprang up and jabbed a finger toward the growing inferno. The idea of managing the barbecue was surprisingly preferable to a grilling from Mom, considering she had a phobia of cooking over an open flame.

Jules swiveled her head over one shoulder and darted to the grill. Along with a series of unintelligible mutterings, she transferred the grease-splattering burgers onto a platter and lifted the dish above her head. "No food for you until you explain yourself. Lord himself knows I didn't raise a daughter to thumb her nose at the law."

A short sigh escaped Maeve's lips. "Nice. Withholding much-needed sustenance from your own daughter. Fine. I can sum up my day as quickly as Calista did hers." She dropped onto a stool and eyed the burgers. "I ate a bag of sugar for breakfast, embarrassed myself and some friends, got myself a new job, made a few headlines, socialized with your sidekicks, nosed around Vic Adams's office, and ran into Detective Taylor. Done."

"Enlighten me." Mom plunked the plate onto the cast-iron table and swung around with her eyes closed, pressing fingertips to her temples. "Why were you in Vic's office?"

The disbelief evident in Mom's tone was understandable. "I thought maybe he killed Trixie, and I wanted to find proof."

"Vic Adams?" Calista's eyes grew wide. "I met him today. He stopped by my booth and picked up a few bottles of perfume for his wife." With lips pursed, she shook her head. "No, sorry. You're wrong."

"How would you know?" Maeve flattened her palms on the counter with an unintentional smack. "You met him once." Here we go. Doubting Calista's sixth sense demolished any possibility of keeping the woman off her soapbox.

"I would've noticed something off about him. Sure, he's a bit weaselly. But a murderer? No."

"Was his wife with him?" asked Mom.

As she shook her head again, Calista fidgeted with

an earring and glanced down. "He was with some guy he kept calling Malone." She stabbed a finger in the air. "Now, that guy? I wouldn't put anything past Malone. He reeked of all things unpleasant."

Malone? That name was attached to a series of shady incidents during Maeve's high school days. Maybe Calista was on to something.

Chapter Seven

The following morning, Maeve braved the reporters trailing her every move and entered The Music Box at precisely nine o'clock. Daphne beat her there.

The mother-to-be beamed a bright smile and patted the larger-than-life bump tenting her orange sundress. "Hey there. Get your training pants on, lady. I schlepped in over an hour ago because sleep, as you might imagine, eludes me these days." She placed both hands on the small of her back and arched with a grimace. "I figured why toss and turn if I could get a head start over here. I've pulled out the nuts and bolts of what you'll need to know. Anything else that arises outside of these details, you'll easily handle on the fly. And if not, just text or call me."

Maeve glanced at the binders, folders, and boxes piled on the antique desk. A solid pit formed in her stomach.

"Wipe the dread off your face. You once knew your mother's antiquated filing system inside and out. Not much has changed." She grabbed a notebook, and several folders piled precariously on top of the paper-and-cardboard mountain slid to the floor.

"Don't you dare." Maeve rushed over, stooped, and retrieved the folders and their spilled contents. "I don't want to risk any excess bending and lifting on your part until I'm good and ready to tackle this monstrosity on my own." She clacked the folders on the edge of the desk and sighed. "I'm filled with all kinds of *why* right now. Why hasn't she moved to an online system?"

"She has. She just doesn't know it yet. Your mother, and you know I love her dearly, but your mother is psychologically allergic to anything having to do with technology." Using both hands, Daphne massaged her stomach. "So, everything you see here is also organized online. In my humble opinion, you're the perfect person to introduce her to the digital world."

Maeve groaned. "Thanks." If Mom despised one thing, it was advice doled out by her impetuous daughter.

****

Three hours later, the oppressive blocks of lead on Maeve's shoulders lifted. In their place, a slight flutter of emerging confidence took hold. If the babies blessed her with a few more days before making their debut, she'd hit the ground running.

Daphne's stomach rumbled a demanding complaint. "Hush." Scowling, she scolded her tummy. "It's not even lunch time yet."

"Actually, it *is* after noon." Maeve giggled. "You'd better feed those two before they stage a revolt. Let's lock up and head over to Happy Beans. My treat."

"We should get a move on." With a grunt, she stood and braced one hand on her hip and the other on the desk, arching her back. "They get pretty busy these days with the girls whipping up their fancy sandwiches. Front door or rear?"

"I wish either option made a difference. I've endured a few of these reporter rodeos before. The trick is to avoid eye contact." She gestured toward the files still sitting on the desk. "Just leave the mess. After we eat, you head home for the day, and I'll take care of everything here."

"You won't have to twist my arm today." Daphne set the alarm and locked the front door. "I'm feeling more tired than usual. At least the heat is letting up."

As they entered Happy Beans, Maeve's heart sank. No way they'd get a table anytime soon with this crowd. A line had already woven itself around the perimeter of the room. Finn caught her eye from the counter and waved her over. "Daph, save us a place in line, and I'll see what Finn wants." Squeezing through the labyrinth of people and haphazard chairs proved more difficult than expected.

"I don't want to start an uproar, so keep a low profile." Finn rounded the corner and steered her away from the servers' door. "Tell Daphne to walk into the kitchen like she belongs there. You go outside and come around back through the alley. I'll let you into the kitchen from there. I'm not about to keep Daphne on her feet waiting for a table for all eternity." He jerked his head toward a clatter pealing behind them, then rested a hand on her elbow. "Duty calls. I'm assuming you don't mind eating in the kitchen?"

"Not at all. I'll see you in a few minutes." After relaying the plan to Daphne, Maeve crept up behind two men of considerable size and used them to shield her exit. She followed the alley to the rear parking lot but stopped in her tracks. An audible gasp escaped her lips.

Baxter Malone stood locked in a compromising position with Priscilla Adams.

She hadn't seen him in years, but Baxter was a mountain of a man. She'd recognize that beefy neck anywhere. And no one elicited a Bohemian flair better than Priscilla at twenty-five. The same observation held true today.

Vic Adams's wife. Maeve stumbled back into the alley and prayed they hadn't spotted her. Several excruciating long minutes passed before two car engines turned over and vehicles left the parking lot. She let herself in through the back entrance to the kitchen. A divine waft of frying onions, bacon, and a hint of maple syrup filled her lungs. She could almost taste the French toast browning on a nearby griddle.

Settled at a tiny card table set against a wall in one corner, Daphne texted on her phone and glanced up at the door squealing open. "I just sent you a message. Did you go for a stroll around the block a few times first?"

What was an appropriate response?

Finn swung in through the door opposite her and, arching one eyebrow, grinned. "Took you long enough. Everything okay?"

"Yeah. Uh, no. I just saw the oddest thing." The gossip mill ran well enough on its own without any help from her big mouth. "It was nothing." Unable to string a sentence together, she maneuvered her way through the narrow kitchen and managed to avoid knocking anything off a counter or cooktop.

After stalling a bit longer to adjust her purse on the back of a metal folding chair, Maeve dared to glance up and found them still waiting. Their expectant stares overrode her inclination to keep quiet. She sighed and rested her elbows on the table. "I shouldn't have said anything. I was just caught off guard. Baxter Malone was out back, and I-I haven't seen him in years."

"Who was he with?" asked Daphne.

The mother-to-be's eyes often glinted with mischief, but something in her tone implied she knew the answer to that question. Maeve paused to choose her words.

"He was with Priscilla Adams, wasn't he?" Leaning back, Daphne clasped both hands on top of her stomach.

Maeve might not like to gossip, but she prided herself on always telling the truth. She wouldn't allow the choices of Baxter and Priscilla to change that fact. "I was in the alley, so my view was from a distance. Are Priscilla and Vic still married?"

"For the time being. The other two are not exactly being discreet with whatever they've got going on." Daphne lifted a finger. "Although, I think there might be trouble in paradise. I was walking by The Pin Cushion a few days ago, and Baxter just about mowed me down leaving the shop. He looked furious."

"So, you knew?" she asked, breathless. She shot a glance toward a stocky man hovering over a stove laden with several sizzling pans. *Please let the cook be too busy to listen in.* "Who else knows?"

"I caught wind of the story while getting my hair done at Tess's. Marsha Blakely was working on a client in the chair next to me. And let me tell you, the woman spilled the whole sordid tale while Marsha bleached her hair to the prettiest shade of champagne blonde I think I've ever seen." After tossing her own strategically placed hints of caramel over each shoulder, she flashed open palms above her head. "Busybody or not, we're talking serious hair color goals. I'm asking for that process at my next appointment. I can promise you that."

A server entered through the swinging door and grabbed a tray.

Daphne paused and waited until she was out of earshot. "Granted, the woman didn't name names, but even a fool could figure out the main players in her story. She started by saying how irked she was that her client took a dress to another seamstress for alterations and likened the betrayal to cheating on your hairdresser."

"Priscilla was the other woman, so to speak?" Swinging a dishrag over his shoulder, Finn crossed the floor in three long strides.

Daphne nodded. "Yep. Miss Champagne Blonde apparently tasked herself with the duty to warn Priscilla on the pitfalls of doing business with her fair-weather friend." She glanced at the exiting server. "Imagine her surprise when she inadvertently barged in on the new seamstress, whom we can all assume is Priscilla, and found her in a quite intimate pose with the town manager. Oooh!" Her eyes squeezed shut, and her bloated, yet still pretty, features twisted. She let out a short breath. "I recognized the woman next to me as a friend of Trixie's. She didn't have many, but I've seen them together a few times at Happy Beans. And I know she's styled Trixie on a few occasions."

"Off topic, are you okay?" asked Maeve. Even for someone who typically maintained a facade of calm during stressful events, the idea of Daphne going into labor right then and there sent her heart into a galloping frenzy.

"Don't mind me." The nonchalant flick of a wrist

conflicted with the clenched fist hovering above her belly. "These two little ladies are making sure I know they're running out of room. Stick to the subject at hand. Gossip's a nice distraction."

"If you say so. Maybe Trixie had a similar encounter with Priscilla and Baxter." Finn's face told her he was thinking the same thing. This possibility provided them both with a motive to ensure the social media darling's silence. Better to keep the theory to herself until she had more information. If alarm bells sounded in Daphne's head, she'd have the story all over town. Maeve needed time to begin digging.

"It wouldn't surprise me," Daphne replied. "Priscilla's shop is right next to The Music Box, and I've seen Trixie go in and out on more than one occasion. In fact, she asked me to reschedule a voice lesson so she could pop over to pick up a dress rather than go all the way home first." The folding chair creaked under her weight. "Don't worry yourself feeling bad for good ole Vic. He's a not-so-innocent victim of the local tittle-tattle. If there's any truth to the whisperings, he and Priscilla have an *arrangement*. Once he's elected to the Board of Selectman, they'll announce an amicable split."

"One dish of dirt at a time, D." Finn dragged over a chair, its metal legs scraping across the floor. "Do you know the name of this blonde fountain of information?"

"Oh, sure." She sat back and rubbed her tummy in wide, lolling strokes. "But I'm not saying another word until you feed these babies. I'm beginning to feel their frustration in the form of massive kicks to my ribs."

A sheepish smile spread across his face. "Sorry, Daph. What'll it be?"

"If breakfast is still an option, I'll have a plate of the Happy Trio, please." Shifting in her seat, she nodded toward Maeve. "The order includes three pancakes, three eggs, and three strips of bacon."

"Comes with home fries and toast." Finn flipped over their mugs and filled one using a pot of regular coffee and the other with the decaf pot.

"Sold." Lack of nutrition took its toll. Rather than waste time stirring in a packet of sugar or a dollop of cream, Maeve lifted the mug to her lips and inhaled the heady aroma of freshly ground coffee beans. One tentative taste led to a gulp of the warm, full-bodied brew. Though she usually preferred the chocolate brownie blend, the rich medium roast took the edge off.

After passing the order to the cook, he returned to the table with two plated jelly donuts. "To hold you over. The rest shouldn't be more than a few minutes. So, where were we?"

Swallowing a deep sip from her mug, Daphne wrinkled her nose. "The countdown is on. I can't wait for a cup of caffeinated coffee." She set down the mug and picked up her donut. "The client was Marjorie."

"Who is Marjorie?" asked Maeve.

"She lives over in Portsmouth. From what I can tell, she is, *was*, Trixie's personal shopper over at Bishop's, and they struck up a friendship."

Finn nodded and picked up a tray of food. "They stopped in Happy Beans together a few times. At least, I'm assuming it was her. She's what you might call flashy." Using his backside, he bumped open the swinging door and headed into the dining room.

"No wonder they got along," said Maeve.

Daphne brandished her donut in the air and shook

her head. "No, not flashy in the same way as Trixie. Trixie liked to be noticed, but everything about her was very high-end fashion modelesque. Marjorie reminds me of a child playing dress-up. Everything's always pink and or sparkly. Including her makeup."

"And yet she's a personal shopper?" asked Maeve. *She's also a potential source for clues*. What secrets did Trixie divulge? Was her ex-bestie aware of any secret fears of retaliation from blackmail victims?

"Well, you know how the fashion world is. Everything's a little over the top, but fabulous clothes come out of it for the rest of us."

Maeve coughed on a swallow of coffee and covered her mouth with a hand. "Daphne, have you met me? When's the last time I gave you the impression I know anything about fashion?"

"Um, never." She spoke through a mouthful of crumbs and coughed on a giggle. "You'll have to take my word for it." Before she could say more, their food arrived. "Oh boy. We're not taking home leftovers today, my friends."

Maeve dug in with overt and audible enthusiasm between bites. The combination of Finn's honey-maple syrup and salty slabs of bacon was perfection. When a triangle of toast remained, she slumped with a sigh and dropped her fork onto the plate. She snorted at Daphne's dish, still half full. "Eyes bigger than your stomach?"

"Please, nothing on earth is bigger than this stomach. Still…" She winced. "I'm surprisingly full."

Exhaustion etched across Daphne's face. "You look uncomfortable."

"I think these chairs are better suited to someone

not toting two extra humans in the belly. I can't get comfortable." She shifted in her seat and wrinkled her nose. "Maybe I will box my leftovers for later."

As Maeve signaled Finn for the bill and a container, she darted her gaze toward his niece Phoebe, breezing in through the back door. She'd grown over the years, but Maeve would know that face anywhere. More striking than beautiful, she had grown into the prominent features which always set her apart.

"Mae!" Phoebe hurled herself across the kitchen.

Engulfed in an embrace fierce enough to knock the wind out of a linebacker, Maeve swayed. Disentangling herself from Phoebe's arms, she stepped back still holding her hands. "Who is this gorgeous creature, and what did you do with little Phoebe?"

"You're one to talk. New York appears to agree with you." She released Maeve and leaned over to peck Daphne on the cheek. "How are you doing this fine day, Mama D?"

"Excellent. But I'll feel even better after a nap." Accepting a paper bag from a server, Daphne stood and headed for the door. Her panting breaths didn't slow her down. "Maeve, thank you for lunch. Nine tomorrow?"

"If you're up to it. Go home, and get some rest." One had to wonder if those babies had other plans today.

"We should get together." Phoebe tugged an apron over her head. "Myra will want to see you, too. Uncle Finn," she hollered over her shoulder. "Do you have plans tonight? We should grab dinner somewhere with Mae."

Maeve shook her head. She'd taken enough of Finn's time. "Or we could just do a girls' night."

"How about my house at seven?" he asked.

The man remained oblivious to her apprehension. "You're not cooking dinner."

"You got that right. I rarely feel like cooking after I close up shop. Plan on pizza."

She'd intended to shrug, but her shoulders twitched in a way that could only be read as flirtatious. Why couldn't she have bumped into Phoebe outside? The conversation took a wrong turn somewhere along the way. Dinner with Finn would open old wounds. And jab at recent ones.

****

Moments later, Maeve rested her forehead on the steering wheel, savoring the mild burning sensation against her skin. Thank goodness for small favors. The parking lot behind Happy Beans was empty. Maybe the scorching afternoon sent the reporters in search of cooler temperatures. Priscilla and Baxter had obviously taken their tryst elsewhere. But not even the sauna level heat in her car eased the tension seizing her body. Maeve could kick herself ten times over. Why did Phoebe feel the need to include Finn in their dinner plans? Why did Maeve agree to go? Why did she have to get all flirty when she didn't even want to be flirty?

When her anxiety flared, she never acted right—always saying something or doing something embarrassing. At visions of Phoebe giving Finn an earful alluding to a rekindled romance, Maeve went rigid. She gritted her teeth and clenched the steering wheel. The urge to march inside and tell the well-intentioned college student to save her breath gnawed at her insides with the unrelenting ferocity of a drill plowing through a wall. Maeve was a mistake Finn wouldn't make again, and she had no business getting romantically involved with anyone in her current frame of mind.

On the verge of hyperventilating, she sat back and closed her eyes. Whoever said meditation was the simple act of focusing on one's breath was either blessed with the attention level of a doctor specializing in long-haul surgeries or was nothing more than a big faker. With little success, she'd tried her hand at the elusive method of relaxation several times but decided to give it another go. As usual, she failed miserably. Someone should award her with the title of meditation failure expert. No shame in being the best at something. Despite a sincere effort, no fewer than one million images and worries flashed through her mind.

Should she mention the affair to Detective Taylor? What if he accused her of placing blame on anyone other than his most obvious suspects? But if Priscilla and Baxter knew Trixie learned of their affair, they had motive. Surrendering to another feeble attempt at mindfulness, she squinted and adjusted the visor. The sun's glare was brutal at this time of day.

She should do a bit of poking around first. Where to begin? She couldn't conjure a reason in the world to strike up a conversation with Baxter Malone. But before moving to New York, Priscilla was a friendly acquaintance. When she took over her aunt's business, Polly's Pin Cushion became Priscilla's Pin Cushion. They got to know each other on a surface level. Situated next door to The Music Box in the center of town, the shop's convenient location provided a turnkey operation.

Maeve sought out the new seamstress on several

occasions for alterations. If she had something needing fixing today, she'd have a reason to stop in. One glance down at her outfit revealed nothing worth mending. *Wait.* Her navy pea coat, sitting in the backseat since April, begged to be dropped off at a dry cleaner. She hauled it over the seat. Turning the sleeves inside out, she offered a silent apology to her favorite fall coat, then gripped the liner with both hands on either side of a seam and yanked with all her strength. The liner tore straight down. She used the same move on an underarm seam.

Satisfied with her handiwork, she hopped out of the car and headed for The Pin Cushion. As she opened the door to the shop, a tiny bell jingled overhead. *Wow!* Priscilla made quite a few changes since taking ownership. Ivory ropes tied back heavy, pink drapes on either side of the front window. Polly's antique sewing machine stood below the windowsill. Racks of clothes lined one wall. Fabric and sewing supplies were organized on shelves along the opposite wall. When Priscilla's aunt owned the place, fabric hung from the bazillion baskets strewn about with no rhyme or reason. The addition of a decorative lamp sitting on the counter and two Queen Anne chairs, upholstered in the same pink shade as the curtains, stood on the Aubusson rug. A trace of vanilla hung in the air.

At the sound of the bell, Priscilla emerged from a back room. "Maeve." She wore a gauzy, floral maxi dress.

With thin strands pulled back on either side of her face and her hair flowing down her back, she evoked an image of an ethereal hippie. Surprise registered in her wide eyes. But her welcoming smile lessened the flurry of activity in Maeve's stomach. Priscilla didn't present as a woman who knew she'd been caught in the act.

"What brings you here?"

"Nice to see you again. I'm hoping you can help me with something." Maeve crossed the room and held up the coat. "The cool weather will be here before you know it, and I'd like to get these tears fixed."

Priscilla took the jacket and studied every angle. "Beautiful," she whispered. "You must have spent something on this piece." She flipped over the jacket and inspected the tears. "Leave it with me, and I'll have it ready in a day or two."

"Thank you." How could she keep the conversation going? Priscilla never feigned interest in other people's business. Small talk was not her forte or Maeve's. The stage was set for an awkward chat. "So, how have you been?"

"Great. It's nice to see you back in town."

As expected, she didn't pry into the why's or for how longs. In fact, she barely glanced up from the tear. "Thanks." To keep from nibbling on a nail, Maeve bit her lip. "I'm planning on staying awhile. With Daphne going on maternity leave soon, I offered to help my mom in her studio."

"I'm sure she's thrilled."

Another person would ask why she wasn't returning to her big city career. Not Priscilla. Maeve was willing to divulge little information without pressure. Instead of waiting for questions, she'd have to do the asking without outright mentioning the affair. To ask if Priscilla killed Trixie was unthinkable. But with a touch of finesse, she could broach the subject. "You've done a nice job redecorating." *Please let her smile appear genuine instead of demented.* "I love this carpet. I feel like I've stepped into a palatial bedroom. And everything is so organized." This time, her words garnered a glimpse of Priscilla's slate gray eyes and a curt nod.

"Thank you. I kept a few of my aunt's touches." She pointed toward the window. "I still have her sewing machine."

The open space in the far-right corner of the room was once home to a trifold full-length mirror Polly swore was from the late 1800s. Now, the area stood vacant. She swept her gaze to Priscilla. "Please tell me you kept your aunt's mirror. I used to feel like a little princess standing in front of it."

Priscilla shifted her gaze to the empty spot and turned back with a rueful smile. "Oh, I keep the mirror in my apartment now. I didn't think it looked quite right in here anymore."

On the verge of suggesting she return the mirror because it would *absolutely* complement the shop, Maeve kept her opinion to herself. Sharing her limited, not to mention unsolicited, decor expertise was a waste of precious time. *Stay the course.* "Terrible what happened to Trixie. And just outside your shop." She gestured toward the rear exit.

Priscilla busied herself with folding scraps of fabric.

Only the quick uptick of one eyebrow and slight twitch of her mouth indicated she'd heard. Maeve rested both elbows on the counter and leaned forward. "Did you know her well?"

"Barely." A muscle in her jaw clenched as she dumped a teetering pile into a nearby basket. "The less time spent with that harpy, the better."

Nothing more than a light swat is ever needed to disturb an angry hornet. "Seems like she had quite the reputation. From what I've learned, her only fans live in cyberspace."

Without looking up, Priscilla continued to fold. "She was all smoke and mirrors."

Maeve almost pitied the material jerked to near shreds. "Did you happen to notice anything strange, or maybe I should say *anyone* strange, in the area on Sunday?"

"Nope. You know the people who live here." She flung a hand to her hip. "Anyone new strolling around, and we all take notice."

"So, you were working that day?"

"Of course. In fact, Trixie was supposed to come in that very afternoon to pick up her cocktail dress." She twisted her mouth into a sneer. "Presumably with a credit card in hand this time. She was planning to wear it to the July Jubilee at the end of the week. I still have it out back. The woman was a shrew, but she had some serious taste. The dress is absolutely stunning."

"Can I see it?" *Anything to keep the conversation going.*

Priscilla paused a beat, then shrugged. "Sure."

Moments later, the unzipped garment bag revealed a gorgeous, burgundy organza gown. Trixie would have looked lovely. Strapless and without any bells or whistles, the exquisite dress needed nothing.

"She was beautiful," Priscilla admitted. "When she first stopped in, the hem was too long and the top too big. On anyone else, the style would have been a little over the top for the occasion, but you could just tell she'd be a showstopper once I finished alterations." Using only her fingertips, she maneuvered the gown into the garment bag and zipped. "I should ask Ryan to pick it up, but I haven't had the heart."

Was that a statement of genuine concern or a performance? She'd have to force an interaction between herself and Baxter, after all. "I don't want to keep you any longer. I'm sure you're busy." Maeve edged toward the entrance. "When my pea coat is ready, just give me a call. No rush."

"See you in a few days." Priscilla returned her smile.

Plodding back to her car, she bowed her head and ignored the unwavering media harassment. Mom would describe that interaction as a dead end. But every bit of information helped. She itched to get her hands on a pen and paper to start a list of what she knew and what she wanted to know before it all ran out of her head. She climbed into the car, popped open the glove compartment, and rifled around.

The sudden knock on her window launched her off the seat.

Chapter Eight

Finn stared into the car.

Maeve's heart leapt, heaving her chest with the force of a bull running at full speed. She turned the ignition, rolled down the window, then clutched her throat. "You scared me half to death."

"Not a funny joke around these parts."

Who's joking? She rolled her eyes. "Can I help you with something?"

"Can you tell me why you're still sitting out here almost an hour after you supposedly left?"

She swiped a damp strand of hair off her cheek and shrugged. "I had a few errands to run." The pencil stuck behind his ear made her heart sing. She pointed. "Can I have that?"

"What?" His fingers tapped the end dented with teeth marks. "My pencil?"

"Please."

"It might cost you."

Eye roll take two.

He laughed and handed over the gnawed pencil.

"Thanks." A napkin on the passenger seat was the closest thing to paper in the vehicle. She balanced it on her thigh and jotted. The lead tore through the flimsy paper, leaving illegible blurs for words and scraping her legs. Why couldn't the man carry smooth, ballpoint pens? For all of the teasing she pelted at Mom's aversion to new technology, Maeve had yet to master some of her cell phone's finest features. But a note-taking app had to beat the chicken scratch on her lap.

"Shopping list?"

She jerked up her head. The sun illuminated the flecks of gold in his copper eyes, squinting at her notes about Priscilla. She held up the napkin, expecting him to laugh at her two-bit policing effort.

"Can I get in?" Without waiting, he rounded the car and climbed inside. His long frame filled the passenger seat. "This is a clown car." He grumbled to himself and searched for a lever.

"Give up the fight. You're about as comfortable as your six-foot-three self will ever be in my vehicle."

"You're probably right." He glanced at her lap. "What are you doing?"

"Just making some notes about the case."

"Why are you getting involved? You're not a detective. Let the police do their job." He raked a hand through his hair. "A freakin' killer is on the loose. You keep nosing around, and you'll end up on his or her radar."

What gave him the right to stick his nose into her business? The fever pitch in his voice matched the crimson creeping up his neck and across his cheeks and set off her defenses. She twisted, but the scooped seat prevented her from facing him head on. "I'll have you know Detective Taylor said my scoop on Vic Adams was helpful."

"What scoop?" Scrunching his forehead, he pressed his back to the door.

He spat "scoop" as if he'd never spoken a viler word. So far, she'd only told Jules and Calista about her trip to the town hall, what she found in Vic's office, and her conversation with Detective Taylor. Although absent from her original list of confidants, Finn was with her now. Sure, he was already fuming. But she needed someone to talk to. "I did a little digging and discovered something that might be important."

With his mouth set in a grim line, he waited.

If anyone else had enough nerve to presume she owed them an explanation, she would respond with a solid *mind your own business*. Instead, the seventeen-year-old still inside her refused to tell him to get lost. "He was hiding money in his office." This was one of those times when learning how to wait a few beats before blurting out inflammatory information would come in handy. Each second of passing silence decreased her ability to breathe in the confined space. She turned the ignition and switched on the air-conditioner.

"How do you know?" His volume just above a whisper, each dragged-out word hung in the air.

"I found it."

"When were you in his office?" He swiped at a bead of sweat trickling down the side of his face, then positioned a vent toward him.

"Last night." When would she learn to bite her tongue? Finn's switch from rapid-fire scolding to slow, deliberate questioning left her unable to swallow over the sandpaper lump in her throat.

"Where was Vic?"

She stared at the back of the building, wishing she'd kept her mouth shut. "He'd left for the night." If she averted her gaze, she could pretend his eyeballs weren't bugging out of his head, and his jaw didn't need a crane to haul it off his chest.

"You were at the town hall after hours? Did anyone see you?"

"A custodian opened his door for me." She snuck a glance. Sure enough, features contorted in shock and horror replaced his boy-next-door good looks. "But he didn't see anything. The cash is hidden in the wall behind a baseboard."

"I'm not even going to ask how you found it." He flopped back against the seat and let out a long exhale. "Didn't the good detective have a problem with you breaking and entering?"

"I don't think so. He saw me leaving and seemed more interested in what I found."

"He shouldn't encourage you."

"I'm coming at the case from a different angle. I just left Priscilla's and—"

"You what?"

The full weight of his stare blazed against her cheek.

"Don't tell me you went over to The Pin Cushion and started cross-examining her."

"Give me some credit." She glanced down at her hands. A few flecks of pink polish remained on one index finger. *Not for long.* Few bad habits were more satisfying, or consoling, than picking off the remnants of an old paint job. "I have a coat in need of some mending and casually mentioned Trixie. She has no idea I know she's seeing Baxter. And when I catch up with him, he'll be in the dark, too."

With knees bumping the dashboard, he struggled to face her. "You cannot talk to Baxter."

"Why not?"

"Because if he trades notes with Priscilla, which is likely to happen, they will both know what you're thinking. You don't know if these people are dangerous."

He had a point, but to give an ounce of credit to his concern would further incentivize the unwelcome lecture. "I'll think of something." She elbowed him and quirked her lips in a half grin. "Maybe I can snoop around his house or office, and you can be my lookout." Finn snapped up his turn to offer a dramatic eye roll, rivaling all of her animated expressions.

"I'd rather not. But do me a favor, and let me know if you don't take my advice. You shouldn't go gallivanting all over town looking for a murderer solo." He opened the door. "I'll see you at seven."

He clambered out of the car with the grace of an elephant navigating a rat maze and stalked toward Happy Beans. Left alone to mull over his opinion, she cranked the radio volume to drown out the words of caution rattling in her head.

She *should* mind her own business—right after she checked out Baxter. Her instincts were usually on target, and the gut feeling about him gnawing at her insides warranted some digging.

****

At seven sharp, Maeve steered into Finn's gravel driveway, a wave of nostalgia washing over her. She'd been with him when he found the sprawling ranch situated on five-and-a-half rambling acres of land. He purchased the property with the expectation she'd move in once comfortable with leaving her mom in an empty house. Instead, she left them both.

She opened the car door and eyed her shoes.

Though the white pebbles added farmhouse charm, they didn't welcome a woman in heels with open arms.

Once upon a time, Finn planned to pave the driveway after completing a few more pressing upgrades.

The women who visited after her departure must have voiced the same complaint. Yet, he'd left the stones untouched.

A spare pair of flip-flops replaced red pumps. She shuffled toward the white fence spanning the length of an empty horse farm. Cool grass tickled her toes, and the cheap sandals slapped against the soles of her feet. For years, they'd shared the same dream of boarding horses, raising goats, and living off their own private farmer's market. The view before her told a story of one man pursuing those goals alone. He probably felt deceived by her sudden departure. She hadn't lied. A part of her once wanted this life. But the other half of her heart longed to see what else was out there.

Despite everything, she was grateful for the life she'd lived the last ten years. Without it, she'd still feel like a country bumpkin, wondering if a more glamorous existence awaited her. And she was happy for a while. Now, she viewed the years spent in the city as a wonderful vacation where every day was a loving-every-minute adventure until a touch of homesickness set in. In the months leading up to her resignation, the excitement of the adventure ceased to exist.

Sure, in the beginning, glittering moments prancing around as Greyson Walker's fiancée were exciting. Another woman would enjoy that lifestyle for the rest of her days without feeling the need to pursue another blessed thing. But as the months droned on, Maeve found herself with too much free time on her hands and spent most of the empty hours reminiscing about her hometown, the people, and the community she cast aside. When the scandal of Greyson and Shannen broke, she had only one place to go.

Tears pricked the back of her eyes. She blinked back the stray drops threatening to escape. Two large, familiar hands fell on her shoulders with a grip offering the warmth and strength of a security blanket. A warm breath caressed her ear.

"As pretty as you remember?" asked Finn.

"Breathtaking." She leaned back into his firm chest. But at the crunch of wheels bumping over the driveway, she pulled away. A swirl of emotions hovered below the surface. Grateful for the interruption, she whirled around and waved at Myra and Phoebe honking their arrival. Spell broken, she laughed and linked her arm through Finn's. "Let's go say hello to your beautiful nieces."

Before the car stopped, Myra's door flung open. She flew around the trunk with arms outstretched.

Once again, a veil of tears blurred her eyes. Unable to keep them in check, Maeve swiped at her cheeks. She missed seeing these two young women grow up and could never get back those years.

"You're squeezing the life out of her, Myra. Let her go," said Phoebe.

Myra released her grip. "She's right. Did I make you cry? I'm sorry if I made you cry."

Brushing away the few rogue tears, Maeve laughed. "Tears of joy. Don't apologize." The stark differences between them always amazed her. Phoebe, with her stick-straight, strawberry blonde hair and large, violet eyes set between strong, angular features, stood close to five foot eleven in bare feet. In stark contrast, petite Myra's cascading, dark hair and darker eyes gleamed in a dainty, oval face. Her flawless, olive complexion shimmered without help from an ounce of makeup.

"Let me grab the dessert, and we'll get this party started." On legs lighter than feathers, Maeve returned to her car and retrieved the two boxes of pastry she'd bought on the way. The bakery was already closed, leaving supermarket varieties as her only option. With a pink box in each hand, she followed the fieldstone walkway to the front porch and passed through the door held open by Finn. She skimmed the ranch's open floor plan. Not much had changed since she'd last been inside. Judging from the enticing scent emanating from the kitchen, something delicious was in the works.

"Sorry for the mess. My nieces invited you to dinner without leaving me time to straighten up."

His tolerance for clutter equated to a single stack of books on the coffee table.

Lifting an eyebrow, she offered a half smile. "Smells like your time was better spent making the appetizers calling me from the kitchen."

"The pizza is due in about forty-five minutes. I knew you'd appreciate something to tide you over." With one sweep of an arm, he invited them into the kitchen and toward an island laden with pans cooling.

Crab dip, nachos, buffalo wings, and three slices of pepperoni pizza later, Maeve tucked into the corner of an overstuffed couch. Two dimly lit lamps cast a comforting glow in the cozy room. A floor-to-ceiling bookcase accented the wall across from the grand, stone fireplace. She imagined herself sprawled out on the plush area rug surrounded by an array of novels before a crackling fire with fat snowflakes falling outside the picture window. The carb overload left her lethargic. In a state of sheer bliss and contentment, she listened to Myra and Phoebe share one hilarious college story after the next. Phoebe's tale of butting heads with the editor of the school newspaper jarred Maeve's memory. "Hey, speaking of newspapers, Finn, I read your article on Trixie's murder. I didn't know you were still writing."

He shrugged. "Just local news, but I enjoy it."

"Have they identified any suspects?" Phoebe flicked a hand in the air and screwed up her face. "I mean, it could be anyone. The woman knew how to push people to their limit."

"So, I've heard," agreed Maeve.

Myra leaned forward and patted her sister's knee. "Remember the time she flounced into Happy Beans and wanted her order on the house in exchange for mentioning us on her website? She phrased the offer as a threat. I believe she said 'if we didn't fork over the free food, she'd shred us on social.' The woman couldn't even keep the few friends she had. And remember when we saw her arguing with Marjorie in the parking lot?" She wiggled her fingers at Maeve. "You should have seen them. They got so nasty. I thought I was on the verge of witnessing some good, old-fashioned hair pulling."

Maeve untucked her legs and placed both feet on the floor. "Do you have any idea what they were arguing about?"

Clutching the armrest, Myra hooted. "Anyone outside within a fifty-mile radius had a front-row seat."

She motioned her water glass toward Finn. "I think you were inside and heard the commotion. Am I right?"

Finn nodded. "Yeah, the bits and pieces I caught sounded like Marjorie was cut out of some deal. I'm assuming the spat had something to do with the new job in New York that Trixie was keeping under wraps."

"I got more than fragments from their exchange." Myra snorted. "Marjorie was downright irate. She made it clear that, in her opinion, Trixie's success was the direct result of her efforts." She shook her head and clanked her tumbler onto the coffee table. "I'm not sure how much truth is attached to the accusation, but I haven't seen them together since."

For the second time today, Maeve listened to rumors of animosity between Trixie and Marjorie. The second half of her day gifted her with a sweet reprieve from the intrusive press, but such good fortune had a finite shelf life. Maybe a few hours alone processing this new information would result in a plausible lead and an end to the allegations lobbed her way.

****

Minutes away from midnight, Maeve drove home, wearing the same grin she'd said goodbye with still on her lips. At the realization, she couldn't stop her smile from growing wider and laughed out loud at herself.

She sketched out another to-do list in her head and prayed to remember most of the tasks once she got home and could grab a pen and paper. Better yet, maybe she'd finally give the dictation feature on her phone a whirl. If she could rattle off her lists whenever the mood or idea struck and not need to worry about writing utensils, life would be so much easier. With her mind veering into virtual assistant land, she risked forgetting a few things.

The hum of an engine rumbled farther up the road. An SUV sped toward her from the opposite direction. The car swerved into her lane, and a combination of glaring headlights and sheer terror blinded her. Every muscle in her chest seized. She gripped the steering wheel and jerked to the right.

The car flew over an embankment and hurtled downhill. She lurched up and down, forward and backward, until the airbag threw her against the seat with a violent blow to the torso. She gasped to replace the air knocked out of her lungs.

When the car finally stopped, she groped for the door handle. Trickles of blood worked their way into her eyes, making it impossible to see in the darkness. The dinner eaten hours ago rose in her throat. Without warning, the door flew open. Two large hands slid under her armpits, gripped bruising shoulders, and dragged her onto the grass. She lowered her head against an unseen, solid chest. After a few gulps of fresh air, she sensed a fraction of the panic easing but struggled to form a coherent thought.

"Maeve?"

That voice.

"An ambulance is on the way."

Grasping for one of the arms still holding her, she used it as leverage to heave herself into a sitting position and squinted through wet eyes at his face. "Detective Taylor?" *Ambulance?* Was she the latest target in a growing list of victims?

****

Maeve's head throbbed with a searing pain she'd never known existed. Her eyes sagged under leaded hoods, but she managed to force them open. A bitter, antiseptic odor induced an overwhelming wave of nausea. The tilting room slid into a hazy focus and stilled. *A hospital room?* An avalanche of memories from her ill-fated drive home stormed through her brain and intensified the headache threatening to render her unconscious again.

A nurse clad in blue scrubs entered. "Look who's awake." The woman observed a monitor and jotted some notes. "I'm April, by the way. How are you feeling?"

April's spring-like curls and gap-toothed smile lit up the room. If she truly wanted to be helpful, she'd pull out a bottle of acetaminophen and bless someone else with her sunny personality. "My head is killing me."

"I can give you something. Your mom stepped out to make a few calls. She didn't want to wake you."

Maeve closed her eyes. A reassuring hand patted her forearm.

"I'll let her know you're awake. The doctor will stop by soon."

The nurse no sooner left than the door flung open.

Please let her stop the madness before it starts. "Mom, I'm fine." She steeled herself for the anticipated onslaught of unanswerable how's and why's, then opened her eyes.

"Fine?" Jules dragged over a chair and clasped her daughter's hand. "Well, I'm glad one of us is *fine*. What on earth happened?"

"Good question." Detective Taylor stood in the doorway behind a grim-faced Calista.

Is it possible for the mere presence of other humans

to increase another person's physical pain? "I don't know. A car in the other lane was moving at warp speed, and the next thing I knew, headlights were coming toward me." She lifted her free hand and pointed a finger in his direction. "You were there."

"I was on my way home from work and watched the car ahead go off the road." Frowning, Detective Taylor stepped around Calista. "Imagine my surprise when I found you at the bottom of the hill."

"Did you see the other car?" asked Jules.

"I did. Streetlights or a moon would have helped, but I can provide a general description." He strode into the room and parked himself on the other side of the bed. Although an empty chair was beside him, he remained standing. "When you're up to it, I'd like you to try and remember what you can and make a statement."

Calista hovered at the door.

For once, she didn't have any otherworldly tips to improve the current state of affairs.

Nurse April entered with a woman wearing tortoiseshell glasses that took up most of her face.

Although cropped to her ears, coarse, salt-and-pepper hair stood on end.

"I'm Doctor Jensen." She offered a curt nod to Maeve. "I've already had the pleasure of meeting your mother. She must be thrilled to see those eyes open."

Did no one have the decency to pass the doctor a bottle of hairspray or a dryer sheet? "How long have I been out for?"

"Hours. You should plan on being sore for a few days."

The last time Maeve suffered an extended hospital

stay occurred decades ago. She was seven years old with a severe case of pneumonia. After four nights of rude awakenings thanks to piercing beeps and nurses popping in to check on her and turn off whatever machine elicited the tortuous noise, she vowed to avoid any future overnight visits. Getting knocked unconscious in a rollover accident superseded all such promises to herself. But the mop-headed little girl still inside begged to escape the glaring lights, continuous drone of various monitors, and pungent stench of disinfectant. "When can I go home?"

"Well, if your guests wouldn't mind stepping out, I can examine you." She flashed a brief smile around the room before settling her gaze once more on Maeve. "Assuming you're well enough, I'm thinking we'll discharge you first thing tomorrow morning."

An exit ticket was welcome news. She loathed hospitals, but the idea of getting out of bed, dressing, and traveling home was exhausting.

No doubt Dr. Jensen intended for the exam to be gentle and brief. But the prodding and poking at Maeve's bruised body lasted an eternity. If less effort was required, she would have cried tears of joy when the doctor left. Every cell from head to toe craved sleep. Heavy lids forced her eyes shut, but a steady stream of images viewed from her cartwheeling vehicle delayed much-needed rest.

She woke to bright, glaring sunshine streaming through the window. What had the doctor said last night? Did she fall asleep during the exam? Fortunately, caring required more energy than she possessed. The whiteboard on her wall told her Betty took over the morning shift. *Hmmm, one doesn't hear of too many people named Betty these days.*

A light rap sounded.

Instead of Betty, Finn creaked open the door. When he saw her sitting up, he opened it fully. "Your mom called. I came right over."

Despite the pain in her jaw, a grin tugged at her lips. "She should have saved you the trip. My head's still a little fuzzy, but I think they said I'm going home this morning."

He removed his phone from his back pocket and sent a text. "I'll save your mom the drive and take you home. How are you doing?"

"Much better. I just want to get out of here." Did she still have a set of wheels? "Hey, how's my car?"

"Last thing on my mind," he said. "I'm more concerned about who put you in the hospital."

"Either a drunk driver or someone using their phone, instead of paying attention to the road." Were his eyebrows drawn together in anger, disbelief, or both? Either way, he wasn't buying her story. Truth be told, neither was she.

"That cop saw the whole thing. Your mother said he claimed the driver purposely ran you off the road."

Did my heart just skip a beat? "Why would someone do that?" She had her own theories, starting and ending with an unidentified murderer running around town.

"Really? After all of your snooping, you don't think someone wants you to butt out?"

Instead of fear, she prickled with anger. With two gentle fingertips, she touched the bandage on the side of her head. Her entire body must be covered in bruises. "So, I'm supposed to just succumb to bullying tactics?

You should know me better than that by now." Memories of the anguish she'd caused Jules over the years was likely the source of his reluctant smile. She was always the first one to intervene at the hint of some perceived injustice. If the bigger, meaner kids had someone in their sights, the small and meek could depend on Maeve to fight their battles. On more than one occasion, she was rewarded with school suspensions for heroic efforts, including everything from shoving a boy twice her size into a bush without knowing a beehive hid inside to vandalizing a prized car with shaving cream and toilet paper topped off with several bags of potting soil. "What are the chances Vic knows I'm suspicious of him? Slim. Priscilla's another story. Baxter Malone better brace himself because he just soared to the top of my suspect list."

Chapter Nine

Rapping sounded on the door less than an hour after Maeve's return home.

Calista left for the expo hours ago.

Mom headed to the studio with assurances she'd be home in a few hours. Strict instructions to stay put until Jules or Calista returned were repeated at least a dozen times.

If it meant putting an end to Mom's all-consuming guilt, Maeve was willing to agree to anything.

Jules perseverated over the fact she'd told Calista to let Maeve enjoy her evening, rather than interrupt dinner with an ominous text harping on some "bad feeling."

Sprawled on the couch with a pillow, blanket, and her favorite home renovation show on the television, she sipped her coffee. The hum of an engine roaring down the street broke the peace she'd almost settled into. Groaning, Maeve boosted herself up and peered out the window. Apparently, some people believed recuperating from a vehicular somersault included unannounced visits from plainclothes police officers.

Seconds later, the doorbell wailed a hideous clang, shattering any progress she'd made toward alleviating a monstrous headache. "It's open!" A searing pain shot through her torso. The sharp stabs ricocheting around her rib cage and abdomen far outweighed the exertion of responding. Still, ignoring him was off the table. With her luck, his next step would entail a concerned call to Jules, setting off a tidal wave of worry. A roar of voices echoed outside.

Detective Taylor let himself in and entered the living room. "How's the patient?"

"Could be better. Could be worse." *Holy hot tamales.* Ignoring how that white shirt enhanced his tan demanded some serious effort.

"You might want to start thinking about keeping your doors locked and not inviting guests in sight unseen." He jabbed a finger toward the window. "The media is chomping at the bit to get a statement."

"Save the safety speech." She hooked a thumb over her shoulder. "I recognized your car."

"You should lock your door." A muscle twitched along his jaw as he knit his brows together.

"Are you here to chastise me, or is there some other purpose to your visit, Detective?"

"I didn't come to socialize." He sized her up and cracked a small smile. "Call me Spencer."

On impulse, she raised an eyebrow and winced under her bandage. "Okay, then. Would you like to sit? I'd offer you coffee, *Spence*, but I'm a bit indisposed at the moment." She flicked a hand at the mug on the coffee table. "Have a sip of mine, if you'd like."

"No, thanks. Let me get right to the point. Based on what I saw last night, the other driver appeared to deliberately veer into your lane."

"You're making an assumption." An echo of Finn's allegation this morning played in her head.

The cushion at the farthest end of the couch sank under his weight. "You don't sound concerned."

"If someone is targeting me, sure I'm concerned. But the person might also drive like a jerk on a regular basis."

"You're more worried than you're letting on." He leaned forward, rested his forearms on his legs, and clasped his hands together. "Any chance Vic Adams learned about your visit to his office?"

"I don't think so." To avoid his intense study of her face, she shifted her gaze toward the television.

"What aren't you telling me?"

Once again, she failed to master the art of crafting a poker face. Giving in, she propped her pillows, sighed, and met his gaze. "I think Trixie found out Priscilla Adams and Baxter Malone are having an affair. I don't think Priscilla could hurt a fly, but Baxter always had a mean spirit. People change, but I wouldn't put anything past the kid I knew in school."

"Don't tell me you confronted them." His jaw set.

The accusation stung. "How dumb do you think I am?"

"I don't remember name-calling."

To prevent further mutilation of her nails, she laced her fingers together and chewed the inside of her cheek. The home renovation experts chattered away on the screen, but she didn't hear a word. A smog of silence swelled in her ears while she waited for him to speak. Except, she'd never been able to tolerate an awkward lull in conversation and tended to fill such gaps with impulsive babbling. "When chatting with Priscilla, I was actually very smooth. She'd never in a million years dream I'm in on her little secret."

Music in a blaring commercial blasted from the TV.

The detective snatched the remote from her lap and tapped the power button with more force than necessary. "Was Baxter present during this conversation?"

"No, Priscilla's fixing my coat." For lack of anything better to do with her restless hands, she braided the tassels on a nearby throw pillow.

"Did she give any indication she saw Trixie on Sunday?"

"Trixie was supposed to pick up a dress after her voice lesson but never showed."

"Do me a favor?"

One line forming between his brows was the single movement in an otherwise rigid face. "What?"

"Stay away from Baxter Malone." He stood and handed her the remote. "I'll be in touch. And try to get down to the station today or tomorrow to make a formal statement about what happened last night."

His buzzing cell phone interrupted the sharp retort sitting on the tip of her tongue. First of all, she worked right next door to Baxter's girlfriend's place of business. How could she promise to avoid him? And second, she already told Spencer everything she remembered. Didn't that information suffice for a formal statement?

Covering the receiver with one hand, he mouthed, *lock up*, pressed the phone against his ear, and let himself out.

A braver man would have stuck around and given her a chance to debate those facts. As she gripped the remote, Maeve shuddered at a sharp twinge radiating down her side. If he thought she was the type to stay silent on the receiving end of a one-sided conversation, he better guess again. Decades of sparring with Mom, reigning champion of word wars, taught her a thing or two about making her voice heard.

Once the ignition turned over, she snuggled under the fleece throw and turned on the television again. The good detective didn't appreciate her conversation with Priscilla, but intuition told her he severely underestimated an angle unrelated to Paige and Seamus. If she could dig up a little something on Baxter, clearing their names was a possibility.

****

A hurricane of energy burst through the door in the form of Jules and Calista with Ida and Luanne bringing up the rear.

Yanked from a glorious few hours of slumber, Maeve propped up her pillow, acute grogginess clouding her head.

Spilling into the room in a flurry of excitement and chatter, they came up short rounding the corner into the living room and gawked.

Maeve scrubbed the grit from her eyes.

"Oh, dear. We've woken you." Luanne bustled over and perched on the edge of the same cushion the detective vacated earlier. "How are you feeling?"

Like I wish you'd leave so I could go back to sleep. The woman wasn't sorry in the least. Guilt, guilt, go away. Luanne meant well. "Better. I was lucky to escape with only a few bruises."

"Lucky?" Jules marched the rest of the way into the room with Calista following at her heels.

Maeve flashed her a warning glare. She already caught an earful from Mom this morning. The detective had no business sharing his suspicions about the other driver with anyone. The last thing she needed right now was for Jules to broadcast that story to Luanne and Ida.

"You must be hungry. Can I get you anything?" Mom asked.

Fortunately, Mom must have understood the tone of her daughter's expression and changed the topic of conversation. Grateful for the opportunity to escape their scrutiny, she uncurled herself from a fetal position and creaked upright. "Thanks, Mom. I think I can fend for myself. It feels good to move after spending half the day on the couch." She glanced at Luanne and Ida. "Can I offer you coffee or tea?"

"We're coming in from lunch." Jules waved her off.

After poking around the refrigerator and making herself a sandwich, Maeve took a bite of the turkey and cheese on rye and turned on her phone. Forty-two text messages waited. Everyone knew what happened and was checking in. Scrolling through the texts, Maeve stopped at a message from an unknown number. She tapped and read.

—*COUNT YOUR BLESSINGS*—

Her mouth went dry, making it impossible to swallow the now-tasteless mouthful of bread. She shoved aside echoes from her earlier conversation with Spencer. The message could very well intend sincere well-wishes from someone in town. But the anxiety creeping up her spine told her the person who forced her off the road still had a bone to pick. She should call the station, but another sermon on staying out of trouble sounded about as much fun as a trip to the DMV. Instead, she nibbled at her sandwich and opened the laptop.

Time to do a little research. She didn't know what to look for but suspected Baxter's social media accounts weren't private. He'd always had a lofty view of himself as some sort of important public figure. A quick search led to his home page, open for all to see. Trolling through photos and quotes exposed only the respectable public servant he wanted everyone to perceive.

At the post confirming his participation in the July Jubilee, she stopped scrolling. The whole town was attending the event, but what other functions had he committed himself to? Tapping the events tab, she smiled. *Jackpot.*

By seven o'clock this evening, he was expected at the grand opening for Sonny's Alehouse.

Heels clicked across the hardwood floor and stopped behind her stool.

"Plans tonight?" Calista asked. "Are you going to Sonny's? Everyone at the expo was talking about it, but you should probably take it easy."

That singsong tone did little to lessen the dull pounding in Maeve's head. But what better place for a random encounter than a restaurant and bar teeming with people? Working up the best doe eyes she could manage, she faced Calista. "True, but I could use a night out. Interested in joining me?" Met with an expression of blatant skepticism, she dropped her gaze to her half-painted pinky finger tapping the counter. If her cover was already blown, why back down now? Besides, she needed a reason to throw on a fresh coat of nail polish. "I'll call Paige, and we'll make it a total girls' night."

"I suspect you'll go with or without me." She

crossed her arms across her chest and smirked. "But I don't relish the possibility of a lambasting by your mother for encouraging you."

She's caving. "Mom has plans tonight. We'll be in and out before she returns."

"I'll go," she spoke slowly, barely moving her lips. "But if you feel the slightest twinge of anything, we're out of there." She rested both hands, lighter than feathers, on Maeve's shoulders. Brows knit together above shrewd pools of sapphire. "And don't think I don't know you're up to something."

For fear of revealing more, Maeve fixed her gaze on the screen until Calista *click-clacked* out of the kitchen. Maybe those hunches would come in handy tonight.

****

A rush of excitement befitting a fifteen-year-old sneaking out of the house surged through Maeve's body. Once Jules's car left the driveway, she dashed to the bathroom. With twenty minutes until Paige arrived to pick them up, the race was on. One shower, a few swipes of makeup, an elastic, a borrowed white tank dress, and she was on her way to Sonny's. The only impediment to an otherwise perfect night was the few cars tailing them.

"You sure you're up to going out?" Paige steered into the parking lot running the length of beach.

"Absolutely. It feels great to get out of the house."

"I hope a spot opens up." The car slowed as Paige craned her neck.

"No rush, someone will leave eventually," said Calista.

Threads of guilt wrapped around Maeve's heart.

Despite sincere intentions to share her plan with Paige, fear took over. The risk of Paige refusing to come was too great. "I see one." She pointed to a truck leaving.

After crossing the crowded boardwalk and dodging several cameras, she climbed a steep set of stairs and stepped into the main entrance filled with a throng of people. A roof covered one half of the restaurant while the other side opened to the night sky. The entire front of the establishment overlooked the beach. In the roaring crowd to their left stood Vic, Priscilla, and Baxter. Nothing like a love triangle to liven up a party.

The years hadn't been kind to Vic. A button-down shirt, which probably fit him at one time, now strained across his protruding stomach. The hem stopped more than an inch above the top of his pants and tented out in a most unflattering way. His bloated face resembled drunken cartoon characters. In stark contrast, Baxter played to his strengths and wore tailored pants and a shirt emphasizing his efforts at the gym. Still, Vic's warm smile outshone Baxter's beady, black eyes and hotter-than-thou smirk any day of the week.

Paige whirled on Maeve and grabbed her arm. "Did you know about this?"

Still sore from the previous night, Maeve yelped.

A flush crept up her neck and onto her cheeks as Paige widened her gaze. "Did you bring me here to spy on these people with you?"

"Of course not. I'm perfectly capable of spying all by myself. And Calista was more than willing to tag along. You're here to keep us company." She smiled at the hostess. "Reservation for three under the name Cleary."

The young woman, dressed in a micro-mini,

fuchsia romper, led them to a square, pub table in the roofless section.

More than one head turned to stare at Calista. In a mass of bronzed shoulders and sun-kissed cheeks, she commanded attention with her shimmering white hair and alabaster skin. The strapless black sundress emphasized every sharp angle of her figure. With an appearance better suited to a high fashion magazine, Calista personified what it meant to stand out in a crowd.

Loud music played, but not so deafening people needed to shout. A band was due to take the stage any minute. The bar and most tables overflowed with people enjoying themselves.

After a server took their drink orders and left them with menus, Maeve tilted her head and scrunched up her nose. "Don't be mad."

"You totally used me." Leaning across the table, Paige narrowed her gaze and drummed fingertips on her forearm.

"Maybe. But only because I want to help you." Maeve steepled her hands under her chin. "I know someone in this crowd is guilty, and I refuse to let you take the rap."

Paige's stiff posture relaxed. "I can't imagine how your little stunt will benefit me, but I appreciate you trying."

Catching sight of Baxter Malone heading toward the restrooms, Maeve slid off her seat. The movement sent a sharp twinge through her torso. She clamped a hand on the back of her chair and stifled a gasp. Any overt signs of discomfort would have Calista and Paige cutting this night short in a nanosecond. "I'll be right back." A bony hand clutched her arm, and sharp nails dug into her skin. Did no one remember she was still in recovery mode? Out of the corner of her eye, she watched Calista's hand dip into her purse.

"Just a sachet with a few sprigs of thyme." Sitting back, Calista jutted her chin toward Baxter. "You're all hot to trot now. But a little boost of courage might come in handy once you're up close and personal with him."

"With who?" asked Paige.

"When I return, I'll fill you in." Zeroed in on her prey, she hustled after him. A tingling rush of adrenaline coursed down her legs.

Without warning, Baxter stopped to check his phone.

Ramming into him, she clutched her seizing heart. She swallowed and stepped back. "Sorry." So much for the cooking spices floating around in her purse. The one thing keeping this man from hearing her now-thundering heartbeat was the din of the crowd. "I-I wasn't paying attention."

"No harm done." Notes of a familiar rock song emanated from the phone in his hand. "Excuse me." He strolled farther down the short hall.

Good manners prevented her from overtly listening to his conversation, so she stepped into the bathroom and held the door open a crack. Making heads or tails out of what he said was impossible, but his tone and hissed words indicated anger and a less-than-pleasant conversation. Yanking open the door, she stumbled into him again. "Sorry, these run-ins are getting embarrassing," she muttered.

Baxter brushed past her, tossed something into a

wastebasket, and stalked off.

Once he was out of sight, she inspected the basket. No need to rummage through trash again. A small white card lay at the bottom of the empty bin. She fished out the card and flipped it over. *Marjorie Banks.* The business logo displayed her name in swirling, purple calligraphy. In bold, purple block print read the title *Designer and Stylist*.

Any inklings of lasering in on Marjorie faded after last night's accident. But this turn of events screamed more than coincidence.

She slid the card into her back pocket and glanced up. If Priscilla's flailing arms and swaying torso were any indication, the woman drained more than a few cocktails tonight. Making small talk lacked an ounce of appeal. But what option existed other than to go over and say hello? Priscilla beamed a blinding smile.

"Maeve, nice to see you again."

This welcome was far warmer than the one offered yesterday. How many cocktails had the woman consumed?

"Have a drink with us." Priscilla hooked a hand around Maeve's elbow and staggered.

"Maybe later. Right now, I'm caught in a time warp. I haven't seen some of these people in years. In fact, I just saw Baxter Malone leaving."

"What?" She scanned the restaurant. "You can't be serious."

Lazy, alcohol-infused eyes turned wild. "He left through that door." Maeve pointed toward the front entrance. "Is everything okay?"

After a long, blank stare fixed on the door, Priscilla puffed out a breath. "Okay? Of course, we're at a party!" She flung out her arms and grazed a server passing by with a tray of drinks.

"Whew! Watch the hands." Paige held up an arm to defend herself and joined them. "Hi, Priscilla. Where's Vic?"

"Weird." Priscilla furrowed a brow. "I couldn't say." A shrug jostled both shoulders and sloshed half the pink contents of her glass onto the floor. "He's around somewhere."

"I'm sure," said Paige. "Maeve, our food is arriving any minute. I hope you don't mind; I took the liberty of ordering a bunch of appetizers we can share and call dinner."

"Sounds great." She turned to Priscilla who once again appeared to lose focus of the people in front of her. "We'll let you get back to your friends. Nice to see you."

Sweeping her gaze along every corner of the restaurant, Priscilla nodded.

At their table, Calista dug into their food with gusto. "Sorry." She chewed and swallowed, a fist covering her mouth. "I didn't know how long you'd take. I'm famished, and this will be an early night."

Maeve learned a long time ago to refrain from asking Calista *why* questions. She never had an answer but was often right on target. Besides, if Calista was correct, time spent eating made more sense than talking. Only the commotion at the front desk had Maeve coming up for air from a plate of the freshest fried clams she'd tasted in years. Was the crispy batter or dill tartar sauce forming her new palate addiction? Noise from the crowd and music playing must have drowned out the sirens, but an unmistakable flash of blue lights glared through the windows.

With grim faces, the staff rushed from table to table.

"I'm sorry to interrupt." The woman who'd seated them adjusted a strap on her romper, then clasped her hands. "Management is asking diners to remain inside while a situation is handled in the parking lot."

"What happened?" Maeve asked.

"I don't know all the details. But it sounds like someone collapsed outside."

As she peered through the window, Maeve felt a shiver run down her spine. Since when were seven police cruisers needed to assist an ambulance call? "Are they okay?" Though she didn't want to miss a second of the activity outside, she faced her current source of information.

The woman shook her head, wide-eyed. "I don't think so."

Not that an unconscious person was good news, but from what Maeve could tell, the incident drew media attention away from her.

Moments later, Detective Taylor entered and stalked toward the manager.

Was it too late to climb under the table? Maeve scoped out every visible exit and prayed for a way to escape without him seeing her.

Within seconds, he glowered from the opposite side of the table.

The shiver she'd felt moments ago had nothing on the torrent of dread rippling through her core.

"Miss Cleary, you must be feeling better."

"I am." Her ears throbbed, keeping beat with her hammering pulse.

"Not well enough to come down to the station for that statement, though?"

"I completely forgot. I took a significant blow to the head, you know."

"I do know." He tapped the table near her cell phone. "Let's put an appointment on your calendar for tomorrow morning at eight. If you set a reminder, you'll be less likely to forget."

She whipped her phone off the table, typed, and held it up. "Great idea."

"Can you tell us anything about what happened in the parking lot?" asked Paige.

He glanced back and forth between them. "I suppose you'll hear about it soon enough. A couple found Baxter Malone unresponsive next to his car. We're not sure what happened yet." He stared at Maeve. "Can I speak to you privately for a moment?"

"Sure." Her temples pounded, but Maeve willed herself to maintain an air of confidence, fixed her posture, and followed him to an empty table in a corner.

"You knew he'd be here tonight." As he tilted his head, a faint line formed between his brows. "Is your goal another ambulance trip to the emergency room?"

Good thing the man chose the police academy over med school. Possessing zero bedside manner, he didn't mince words. "You're making a pretty lofty assumption. We were hungry and had every right to check out a new restaurant."

"Stop." He held up a hand. "You're here to see Baxter. Before I get into the zillion reasons why that plan is wrong, I must ask if you engaged with him or anyone else in his party."

Did she dare ask him to elaborate on what he

meant by *engage*? A few mumbled apologies for barreling into someone couldn't possibly equate to a conversation. "I wasn't planning to. I wanted to come and watch from afar. See if anything odd jumped out."

"You didn't answer my question."

Nope. She didn't. But what were the chances of this guy allowing her to leave without coming clean?

After relaying the series of events that happened since bumping into Baxter, she breathed out. Avoiding the frustration reflected in his eyes grew impossible. "You can stop looking at me like I'm your biggest headache. I'd dare say I've been helpful." She sniffed.

He stood. "*I'd* say you should head home and get some rest. I'll see you in the morning."

Her cellphone chimed the arrival of a new text message from Mom. Finally, an opportunity to ignore the exasperation screwing up his face. Daphne gave birth to two healthy baby girls. Without the new mother to continue showing her the ropes, she needed to get an early start tomorrow.

Stopping by the police station would make for a long morning, but maybe she'd hear an update on Baxter's condition. At the very least, he just moved from the suspect list to the victim list.

Chapter Ten

The Music Box's closed drapes and locked door sent the clear message of *get lost* to prying eyes. Maeve sat alone and stared in disbelief at the numbers on the screen. During her brief training with Daphne, overwhelmed with what and where everything was, she didn't have time to delve into the information. Was Mom paying attention? She'd never mentioned any problems. The decline in revenue traced back to the renovations made two years ago.

Jules spared no expense. Perhaps she assumed they'd recoup the money with an uptick in clients seeking an updated music studio. Instead, the number of students remained flat while unexpected expenses crept up. They needed to find a way to draw in more students.

The prospect of broaching the subject with Jules seized her neck and shoulders with tension. Mom might resent someone telling her how to run her business. Especially someone she'd employed for only a few days. That upcoming conversation, in addition to the earlier discussion with Detective Taylor, would round out a less-than fantastic-morning.

Her descriptions of the other car and the series of events matched the details recorded in Spencer's own statement. But the mention of the text received the following day just about set his hair on fire. That text left no doubt in his mind the other driver purposely caused the accident, and he couldn't understand why she hadn't told him sooner.

Despite the annoyance of yet another litany of reasons for staying out of the investigation, she stumbled onto a piece of interesting information at his desk.

A woman had approached with a handful of files. Placing them on the desk, she knocked over a container of pens and pencils. Butterfingers caught the container but swiped several manila folders onto the floor, spilling the contents next to Maeve's seat.

When Maeve hopped up to help retrieve the papers, she spotted the name Baxter Malone. One word jumped off the page—*assault*. A quick scan of the document revealed the case remained unsolved. While still digesting that little nugget of information, she exited the station and walked smack into a roadblock of news outlets, demanding to know if mere coincidence landed her at another crime scene.

Now, with the studio dim except for the light cast from the computer's screen, silhouettes of varying sizes and shapes paced outside. Dare she peek at today's headlines? Only if she craved a bitter blow to the few wisps of serenity remaining in her life. The four lesson cancellations for today provided enough information. But one press of a key shredded any hope of untangling her name from a growing list of dreadful events. Between the decrease in revenue and the business's ties to the negativity surrounding her daughter, would Mom manage to keep the school afloat?

In the silence, the jarring of the doorknob stopped her heart. She froze. After a gentle click, the door slid open and brightened the room with a burst of morning sun.

"Someone is off to an early start." Jules breezed into the studio dressed in tight gray pants and black strappy sandals. Today's cooler temperature inspired a lightweight, cream peasant blouse. A few bubblegum-pink-tipped strands framing her face escaped the silver hair piled on her head. "Do you have a good reason for sitting in the dark?"

"Are you in possession of a superpower that allows you to ignore the obvious? I have enough distractions without worrying about a bunch of onlookers peering in."

"They'll tire of you sooner or later."

"I think they're leaning more toward later after what happened to Baxter last night." She took a breath. "Do you have a minute?"

Jules glanced at her phone. "My first lesson is in twenty minutes. What do you need?"

Undeterred by the time constraint, Maeve waved her over so they could view the screen together.

"You know I prefer paper." Grimacing, Jules grumbled to herself but strode toward the desk.

"I know. And all this information is in the filing cabinet for you to peruse at your leisure. Humor me for a moment."

After a single glimpse at the highlighted items on the screen, Jules held up a hand. "Maeve."

Great. Once the mother-knows-all tone is invoked, the wall was up.

"You've worked here for how many hours?" Jules chuckled and shook her head. "I've already gone over these figures with Daphne, and I'll tell you what I told her. Businesses have their ups and downs. I'm not a bit concerned. Your time would be far better spent familiarizing yourself with the day-to-day routine. Discussion closed." She opened the piano and sifted through sheet music. "By the way, Luanne was kind enough to drop me off and will give me a lift over to Aspen Commons in a few hours. But you'll need to pick me up at two. I hope you sort out your car situation in the near future. I'm used to coming and going as I please, you know."

"I'm trying, Mom. The car's totaled." Affording a replacement in the short term might prove impossible. To make matters worse, opting for the lowest premium, Maeve had lacked the foresight to purchase the optional rental car coverage offered by her insurance company. Now, she lacked the funds to pay out of pocket, even if a hope and a prayer existed for potential future reimbursement. But that detail belonged under lock and key for the time being. No need to worry Mom with yet another mishap in her daughter's life that she'd end up shouldering the weight of.

A girl of about fifteen, wearing long braids and denim overalls, entered. "Morning, Mrs. Cleary."

Saved by the bell.

"Come on over, Gina," said Jules. "Say hello to my daughter. Maeve is filling in for Daphne while she's out on maternity leave."

After nodding a quick greeting, the girl got down to business on the piano.

Maeve listened, astonished by her talent. Though tempted to sit and watch, she busied herself with a string of emails and waited until the thirty-minute lesson was over to comment. "Gina, that song sounded fantastic. How long have you been playing?"

"Five years."

"She's a natural," added Jules. "Gina has an ear for music. If you're still around this winter, you'll have the pleasure of attending her performance at the Snowflake Showcase. Her pieces are never short of perfection."

One lesson led to another, and the morning flew by. By the time Paige arrived, Jules was ready to leave for Aspen Commons to perform her monthly sing-along. She'd been visiting the retirement home since Maeve was a child.

"Luanne's out front," Paige told her.

"Thanks." Jules shot a glance at Maeve. "I'll see you at two."

"I'll be there." As the door closed, Maeve stood. "This morning, I confirmed Baxter's attacker is still on the loose."

"I wish I hadn't agreed to go last night." With lips turning down, Paige swallowed. "Ending up in the same vicinity as another crime was a real boon to my case. How am I supposed to focus on my lessons after hearing that news?"

Her words fell in a weighted blanket of truth smothering any potential reassurances. In one night, the promising prospect of pinning Trixie's murder on Baxter disintegrated. Would the police now attempt to link Paige to both attacks? How long until they viewed one too many online allegations against Maeve and set their sights on another innocent person?

****

Twenty minutes ahead of schedule, Maeve entered Aspen Commons, hoping to catch the end of the performance. Unlike the sterile atmosphere of similar establishments, this building's foyer welcomed guests and residents into a cheerful space bathed in sunlight and adorned with a variety of flowering plants. A chemical blend of bleach and medication was muted by the more pleasing combination of citrus and cinnamon.

With a phone pressed against her ear, the receptionist gave a short wave.

From the front desk, Jules's deep, melodic voice, joined by several others, poured down the hallway. Maeve followed the music along the familiar carpet.

The doors to the common room stood wide open, revealing a large audience of residents and staff. Maeve remained unnoticed in the hallway and pinpointed the theme for the day as music from the fifties. Some members in the audience clapped and tapped their feet, while others sang along. As she hummed, the glimmer of an idea took shape.

Why was Mom waiting until December for a student performance? Sure, newer students might feel uncomfortable on stage. But what about Gina and clients with similar skill levels? Since the inception of the business, The Music Box held two performances each year. The Snowflake Showcase collected donations for the local food bank, and the annual recital in June allowed students to demonstrate their growth over the year.

Perhaps more opportunities to perform would increase business. Residents here often referred grandchildren to the school. Plenty of events and venues welcomed free entertainment. And performing in front of a live audience offered a valuable skill for the students. She suspected many students would love it. They could perform solo or form a small band.

Didn't every kid, at some point, dream of joining a band?

The annual July Jubilee flashed before her. Surely some students would agree to perform a brief piece they'd already learned. What better advertisement for the school? Furthermore, Paige and Jules could bring a few instruments and offer mini lessons. Her mind raced through ideas until the crowd roared with applause. Now to pitch the idea to Mom. Would she welcome a viable suggestion to increase business or resent the implication that she'd lost her entrepreneurial touch?

****

Swinging into Jules's driveway, Maeve came up for air.

Once the car shifted into Park, Mom stared for a moment. "Are you finished?"

Bracing herself for a firm rejection, Maeve nodded. "I am."

"I like it."

Maeve opened her mouth, but the unexpected approval stole her words.

"I don't know how many students are willing to give an impromptu performance in a few days, but I know some will love the idea. And I think many more will want to participate going forward. You're still learning the ropes, but between you, me, and Paige, we can give your idea a try." She smiled. "Close your mouth, dear. Gaping never flattered anyone, and Finn just pulled up." She hopped out of the car, gave a cursory wave to Finn, and let herself into the house.

Maeve sat, unable to even remove her key from the ignition. When in her life had Mom so readily agreed with something she'd suggested? Jules's standard replies were always, "Yes, but maybe this…" or "Sure, but perhaps that" or "It might be better if…." Never a simple "I like it." Where in the world did this change come from?

At the rap on her window, she lurched in the seat. Finn's scowl was a fair-weather welcome home. For lack of better options, she turned off the car and climbed out.

He leaned toward her, every cord in his neck bulging. "When were you planning to tell me?"

"Tell you what?" As if she had to ask. Baxter's attack was headlining news.

He arched back and exhaled a sharp breath. "You witnessed an attempted murder?"

"I didn't *witness* anything," she scoffed. "And who said anything about murder? We could be talking about an attempted robbery."

Lifting his gaze and shoulders toward the sky, he took a deep breath and exhaled. "From what Paige told Seamus, and Seamus told me, you went looking for trouble last night and found it."

"Don't be so dramatic." The truth in his words chafed. But the twinge of guilt prickling her insides stemmed from the nearly imperceptible quaver in his voice as his words trailed off.

He followed her up the stairs onto the front porch and joined her on the rickety swing.

The swaying momentum eased the faint throbbing in her temples. The swing had seen far better days when they were kids, but the whining rhythm imparted a measure of peace. "I was at the police station this morning. Paige is their prime suspect."

"How do you know?"

"Her picture is hanging on a board behind Spencer's desk. Others are also on display, but hers is off to one side all by itself."

"You need to stop nosing around." His lips twisted. "And he's *Spencer* now?"

"Can we stick to one topic?" A cool, late afternoon breeze ruffled her hair. Right about now, she could use a light sweater. She was probably the only human in town begrudging the dip in temperature.

He raked both hands through his hair and groaned. "Fine. I don't see the significance of the picture."

Was he making a conscious effort to play dumb? "According to her own statement, Paige was the last one to see Trixie alive. She maintained a relationship with her old boyfriend, who was engaged to Trixie. To someone who didn't know her or their current relationship, jealousy was the most obvious motive."

"I don't buy it. Why would she put the body in a dumpster right outside her place of business?" He threw up his hands, disrupting the motion of the swing. "And how would she even get her inside there without help?"

She brandished one index finger in the air. "Those unsolved mysteries bring us to Seamus. He didn't admit to seeing Trixie, but he was in the right place at the wrong time." Slumping, she let her head fall back and inhaled a clarifying breath infused with the petunias flanking either side of the swing mingled with a hint of Finn's musky cologne of woodsy tones and coffee beans. "And Trixie accused him of stalking her. I think he and Paige should come clean. They're each other's alibi. But they already withheld information, so I don't know if the admission will make things better or worse."

143

As Finn pressed his heels down and released, the swing creaked forward and back. "My money's on Vic Adams. I don't know what motive he'd have for killing Trixie, but who else had a reason to attack Baxter? Daphne insinuated the marriage was a sham. But maybe he cared about the affair if for no other reason than she'd embarrassed him."

"I wouldn't be so sure." She pulled up her legs and hugged both knees to her chest. "I'm not convinced he knew about Baxter and Priscilla. You didn't see him last night. He positively glowed with happiness. She was the one acting strange."

"How so?" He slowed the swaying motion and shifted to face her.

"I'd say she was agitated." One finger traced the grains etched in the wooden arm. "Granted, she had too much to drink. But she was disturbed Baxter left without saying goodbye." She let out a short breath. "I was so sure he'd go to extreme lengths to keep Trixie quiet. In high school, that man had the moral compass of a cockroach."

The crack of an ancient window opening on the second floor reverberated above.

Finn placed both feet down and stopped the swing's movement. "Well, he's off the hook now."

"Is he? I overheard him arguing on the phone."

As he stood, the swing shook. "So?"

"I have reason to believe he was talking to Marjorie." She craned her neck and lifted a hand to shield the sun glaring into her eyes. "Most of the conversation didn't make sense. But he dropped her business card into the trash. Naturally, I jumped to the most obvious conclusion."

He quirked up one corner of his mouth, producing the faintest smattering of laugh lines on his right cheek. "Sounds like you were dumpster diving again."

His smirk calmed the beehive stirring in her stomach. "Not funny."

"I'm sure the police are already looking at his phone." He cleared his throat and changed the subject. "How are you feeling?"

"Fine. I'd feel even better if I could get my hands on a new car." She clasped her hands together and lifted them to her chin. "Well, used. But new for me."

"I can help." Both hands thrust into his front pockets, and he rocked back on his heels. "My mom's car has lived in my garage for almost a year."

"Why haven't you sold it?"

He stepped away and rested his forearms on the porch rail. "I haven't been able to part with something she spent so much time in. If I try hard enough, I can sit inside and still smell her perfume." As he tilted his head up toward the sky, a small smile touched his lips. "Sound ridiculous? Who gets sentimentally attached to a car, right?"

"Not at all. Think about how many hours a year most of us spend in our cars. I always felt like mine had a personality."

"Exactly." Nodding, he grinned.

The sympathy card she'd sent hadn't been enough. Nothing more than foolish pride kept her from attending the funeral. She swallowed over the tightening in her throat. "I'm sorry I didn't make it to the services."

Staring at the street, he shrugged. "We'd lost touch. I didn't expect to see you there."

Unexpected tears blurred her vision. She tipped back her head and blinked several times. "I should have come. Your mom always went out of her way to make me feel like part of your family. Regardless of what went on between us, she was important to me. She was a beautiful person, Finn."

"I know." He inhaled a sharp breath and faced her. "So, the car's about ten years old. My mom put quite a few miles on it, but she kept up with maintenance. Are you interested?"

A million yesses. Another mom might not have wanted the woman who broke her son's heart to take ownership of her car. Had she been disappointed? Probably. But the Stella Keaton she remembered never had a judgmental bone in her body. "How much do you want?"

"Nothing."

"I couldn't." A lump lodged itself in her throat.

"Yes, you can. And I honestly think she'd be happy to see the car go to you. You might need a few things checked or tweaked before you put the wheels on the road. I'll set up something with my mechanic."

Unable to swallow, she coughed and ventured a wobbling smile. "I don't know what to say." Her voice trembled on the last word, but she forced herself to continue. "I don't feel right about accepting such a large handout."

With a fleeting glance over his shoulder, he bounded down the steps. "Well, I do. I'll give you a call tomorrow." Using long, quick strides, he cut across the grass.

Her throat, tight with unshed tears, burned. An avalanche of the consequences of every mistake made over the last ten years crashed over her shoulders, releasing a tidal wave of regret and sorrow. Every bad decision stemmed from leaving Finn. That single, unalterable choice planted a weed now threatening to overtake her last thread of self-preservation.

****

The doorbell blared a more-than-welcome arrival throughout Jules's house.

"Pizza's here," Maeve hollered. Starving, she yanked open the door, expecting to see someone carrying two large pie boxes. *Come to Mama.*

Instead, Greyson peered through the screen. "Sorry, I forgot to pick up dinner."

She stood frozen in place with a series of options flashing above his head. Slam the door in his face? Slap him? Tell him exactly what she thought of him? Since the morning of the famed incident with Shannen, she ignored every call and text.

"Can I come in?" Unblinking eyes stared from a solemn face.

"I don't think so." With an ounce of luck, she infused the same ice into her voice that coursed down her spine.

"Give me five minutes?"

He doesn't deserve five seconds. She stepped onto the porch and tugged the door closed behind her. A light evening breeze lifted a few tendrils of hair from her face. "I'll give you 'til my pizza's delivered." *Please let the driver show up any minute.* "What are you doing here?"

"I've been in town a few days, working up the nerve to see you."

"Oh, you do have some nerve." She crossed her

147

arms over her chest. To think she'd once imagined herself the luckiest woman in the world to have Greyson Walker choose her. The slightest attention from him never failed to steal her breath. The world almost seemed brighter in his company. Perhaps it was the haggard sag of his chin or the uncharacteristic touch of dishevelment in his overall appearance, but whatever the cause, not an ounce of desire remained. Gone were the quickening heartbeat, the tingling nerve endings, the impulse to clasp his hand, or touch him at all. "What a waste of a long trip. I want nothing to do with you."

With lips sliding into a thin line, he rocked back on his heels, plucking his thumbs through his front belt loops. "Full disclosure, I'm in town on business. My plans fell apart, but I stuck around for a few days, hoping to find the courage to reach out."

"What business could you possibly have in Hampton?"

"We were set to hire a new fashion and lifestyle host. I accompanied a small crew to film a few introductory pieces promoting her as a small-town girl with big ideas." He rubbed the back of his neck. "Craziest thing, though. Someone murdered her."

Wordless for a moment, Maeve stared. "Trixie's glamorous new job was working with you?"

He jerked up his head, widening his gaze. "You knew her?"

"Do you think there's a soul in Hampton who didn't?" The sight of him moving to sit, uninvited, on the porch swing sparked a flare of hot anger in place of her original frigid reception.

"Good point."

Although enough room remained on the seat, she

stepped back and leaned against the railing. "Where's the new love of your life?"

As he set the swing in motion, the floorboards moaned under the weight of his shoes. His head dipped, and he ran his palms over his thighs. "Shannen and I are over."

"So soon?" *Please let my sarcastic tone of mock sympathy ring through loud and clear.*

"She got it into her head I was coming to Hampton to get back together with you and paid me a surprise visit. But Trixie met me for a business lunch at my hotel. Shannen showed up, got the wrong impression, and pitched a fit."

"Poor thing." She flattened a hand against her chest and jutted out her lower lip. If he sought a sympathetic ear, he set his sights on the wrong woman. But the impromptu visit and tale of woe proved he was oblivious to that fact.

"Fortunately, we were alone, and I escaped the altercation without the scene making the tabloids. I think Trixie was pretty shaken, though. Shannen is intense."

"Don't look to me for reassurances."

He shook his head. "She stormed off without giving me an opportunity to explain the situation, and I haven't heard from her since. Much like you, she's avoiding my contact efforts." He shrugged. "We weren't on solid ground, anyway. She was never supposed to be a long-term relationship."

Odd how at one time, the thought of Greyson's involvement with another woman would have set off a burning flash of jealousy. Now, only the urge to escape his self-absorbed, suffocating presence battered her chest. The man refused to see beyond his own unjustified suffering. "It sounds like you've overstayed your welcome in town. When do you leave?" And when will the words stop tumbling out of his lying mouth? For all his talking, he might as well engage in a conversation with himself. Only now did his gaze appear to focus on her face.

"My crew left Tuesday. I'm overdue."

In danger of fleeing into the house before hearing him out, she leaned back and gripped the railing with both hands. A show of strength was of utmost importance. "If you're waiting for me to give you a reason to stay, don't hold your breath." Finally, the hurt crossing his features revealed a glimmer of recognition that his visit was unwelcome.

"When are you coming back?" He cocked his head to one side. "All your things are still in the apartment, constantly reminding me how badly I screwed up."

At that moment, her future became clear. She wanted to stay in Hampton permanently. Nothing and no one pulled her back to the city. "I'll make arrangements to return and pack my things."

"You don't understand." He stood, knitting his eyebrows together. The swing squealed to a stop. "I don't want you to move out."

Unintelligible music blasted up the road moments before a pizza delivery car roared to the curb in front of the house.

"Time's up."

Accustomed to doting fans bending to his will, he set his jaw. Grateful for already paying online with her credit card, she handed the driver a tip in exchange for the pizzas and let herself inside without another word.

To reinforce the finality of her goodbye, she slammed the door.

Jules waited on the edge of an island stool in the kitchen.

"I can tell by your face you know who was here." Maeve set the boxes down on the kitchen table. She opened the lids, and a delicious whiff of tomato sauce, melting mozzarella, and toasty dough wafted up. For once, Greyson failed to impact her appetite.

"It took everything I had to restrain myself from going outside and giving that pompous snake a piece of my mind." Holding two plates, Jules joined her at the table.

"I had it covered." Cheese, heavy with pepperoni slices, dripped over the sides of the crust, burning her fingers. Transferring a square of the Sicilian-style buffalo chicken to her plate was less messy. "Are we supposed to wait for Calista?"

"No, she had dinner plans with some people from the expo." As Mom lifted a slice, strings of cheese stretched from the box. "Let me guess. He wants you back?"

Maeve paused mid-bite and lifted an eyebrow. "Isn't that always the way?"

"It doesn't sound like you gave in."

The hint of a smile playing on Jules's lips likely had nothing to do with the slice of buffalo chicken in her hand. "You know me better than that." The first bite of cheesy goodness burnt the roof of her mouth. "And I made a decision. I'm not going back to New York. If you'll have me, I'd appreciate it if I could stay here until I get my feet back on the ground—financially."

Jules beamed. "Your company's been a welcome

change. I don't miss rattling around in this big old house alone."

At risk of scalding a few more taste buds, Maeve blew on her slice and tried another bite. A soft chunk of blue cheese muted the intensity of the sauce while still allowing a sinus-clearing percentage of spicy heat to break through.

"Daphne called earlier. She gave her notice."

"What?" Not that this news should come as a shock. But picturing an ocean without fish was easier than imagining The Music Box without Daphne.

"Paying for daycare for two infants doesn't make sense. Her salary simply isn't enough to offset that expense." Mom gave a watery smile. "I think my heart's breaking a little, but I'd never tell her." Setting down her crust, she exhaled a deep sigh. "I know having your mother for a boss isn't ideal, but the job's yours if you want it."

"Thank you. I feel like an enormous weight's been lifted."

Jules blinked away the dampness forming in the corner of her eyes and pushed back her shoulders. "Good. Now you can get going on that idea you had for arranging some performances. I sent out a mass email to gauge interest in performing at the Jubilee and received a surprising number of positive responses in the short time we've been home. You might want to think about organizing a lineup."

Leaning in, Maeve fanned out her fingers and pressed the palm to her chest. "But so many people cancelled today. I was afraid they were starting to believe the slanderous reports about me."

"*Please.*" After dropping a half-eaten piece of crust

onto her plate, Mom selected another slice from the box. "Some of the parents thought it best to resume lessons in a week or so, once the fanfare outside the studio dies down."

A fluttering stirred in her abdomen. If the show was successful, a whole new direction for the business was possible. "I'll get to work right after we clean up."

Jules chuckled. "Tomorrow. You're off the clock."

The glob of tomato sauce on one finger demanded she disobey a Cleary cardinal rule of etiquette. She popped the finger into her mouth, then wiped her hands on a napkin. "I can't wait to get started. And the show is a productive outlet to take my mind off Greyson." She widened her gaze. "I didn't even spill all the details yet."

On the verge of launching into the story, she snapped her mouth closed. Why was Shannen avoiding Greyson? Her heart skipped a beat. Was Shannen angry enough, unhinged enough, to hurt Trixie?

Chapter Eleven

The shrill alarm woke Maeve from a sound sleep. With eyes still closed, she patted around until she found the off button. Burrowing under a blanket, she cracked open one eye. According to her smart watch, she accumulated fewer than four non-consecutive hours of sleep. *Those cats. That door.*

If she did nothing else today, she'd find something to prop against the door to keep it closed. One after the other, Mom's cats barged in throughout the night with the sole purpose of sharing her pillow. Medication usually kept her allergies in check, but sleeping with a cat on her head begged for trouble. Thanks to the new possibility of Shannen's motive for murder, the ever-changing list of potential suspects played a role in Maeve's insomnia. But the ability to breathe in bed might give her a fighting chance at a few hours of rest.

Groaning, she dragged herself from the bed. No sense complaining to Jules. She waited a long time to welcome cats into the house. When Jules learned one-year-old Maeve's chronic sneezing and itching were attributed to the family's beloved Sugar, she gave the lap cat to a friend. Although brokenhearted, she refused to resort to medicating her young child for the sake of owning a pet. The next kitten, Mittens, moved in less than a week after Maeve's departure for New York. Jules declared Maeve's adult body capable of tolerating allergy meds if she wanted to visit. With Dad gone, who could argue with that logic?

After a lukewarm shower, the donning of an ancient sundress, and a cup of coffee, she allowed a fraction of the sluggishness to wear off. A note scrawled in Jules's impeccable penmanship stated the car was Maeve's for the day. Outside, a lawnmower rumbled to life and interrupted the quiet of the house. Maeve rummaged through a drawer for a pad of paper and pen to record the details bearing some of the responsibility for her lack of sleep.

She flipped from one page to the next, writing each potential suspect's name. After tearing out the pages from the small stack of paper, she spread each sheet on the hardwood floor. Pen in hand, she scanned her handiwork and jotted notes under the names.

Without a doubt, Paige and Seamus were innocent. Ryan was unaccounted for, but she believed him innocent, as well. Next question, why was Vic hiding money? Did those details have anything to do with what happened to Trixie and Baxter? Baxter was her prime suspect, but she'd gone down the wrong rabbit hole on that one.

Was jealousy a valid motive for Shannen? So far, the fashion influencer repelled all but two humans. Priscilla built a fledgling professional relationship with her. And Daphne described Marjorie as a *friend* of Trixie's. Maybe one or both could tell her more. Better yet, a glimpse into their social media stories might prove useful.

First things first. She better get over to The Music Box and contact student performers with the tentative schedule created last night. Touching base with a few local venues and coordinators of upcoming events would lock in some dates for future performances. And a poster board with upcoming show dates displayed at the Jubilee might help to increase interest in the school.

She grabbed the pad of paper again, flipped to a clean page, and made a quick list including Aspen Commons, The Harvest Fair, Trick or Treat on Main Street, and the library's annual sidewalk sale. At a minimum, she'd plan two events for October and two for November.

After rinsing and depositing her mug in the dishwasher, she stuffed the sheet of potential venues into her pocketbook and slipped on a jean jacket. Her stomach grumbled a complaint. No time for breakfast. Now to stash the pages with names and notes into the antique mahogany secretary's desk. She headed for the living room. Spencer's hulking figure loomed through the screen door. What was he doing here? Would it kill him to give her a heads-up just once before materializing on her front porch uninvited? Even her closest family members and friends had the courtesy to call ahead.

"I was just about to knock. May I come in?"

She darted her gaze toward the room opposite the foyer. Could she steer him in the other direction? "Sure."

He followed her line of vision and glanced into the living room. Skipping the formalities of a morning greeting, he strolled past and eyed the papers strewn about the floor. After taking in the sight before him for several moments, he spun on a heel and leveled her with a hard stare. "Looks like you've been busy."

Maeve opened her mouth to speak, then clamped it

shut. No sweet talking her way out of her makeshift suspect list. Any police officer unable to figure out what she'd been up to required a second stint in the academy. Still, how dare he crouch and read her private notes? She resented her stomach twisting into a jumbled hornet's nest. A few scribbled words didn't equate to meddling in police business. She bit back the urge to inform him of this obvious fact.

He stalked across the room.

All oxygen vanished from her personal space.

"Do you honestly not care that every minute you spend digging up clues puts you in increasing danger?" A line etched between his eyebrows, and the sliver of a vein protruded from the center of his forehead. "Do you have such little regard for your own safety?"

Maeve swallowed through the tightening vise clenching her throat and stepped back. "I haven't done anything wrong." She gestured toward the floor. "Those pages are just me thinking in ink. Now, can you tell me what brought you here? I need to get to work." Noting his narrowed gaze, she backed up another step.

"Good morning, Detective." Calista stood at the top of the stairs. She wore a tight, black halter dress with mile-high sandals and had twisted her white hair into a severe bun on top of her head. Not a baby hair fell out of place.

"You were at Sonny's Alehouse opening," he said. "But I don't think we met."

"Not formally." Taking one casual step after another down the stairs, Calista flashed a wide smile. "I'm Calista, Maeve's cousin." On the landing, she rested a hip against the newel post. "What brings you by?"

He slipped a hand into his pocket, extracted a silver hoop earring, and turned toward Maeve. "I believe this is yours."

"My earring. Did it fall off when I was at the station on Monday?" Though her ears were bare, Maeve lifted a hand and touched an empty lobe. "I never noticed. Thank you."

"Very sweet of you to play deliveryman." Again, Calista grinned. "I'm sure we'd love to offer you some coffee, but we're both heading out."

If the irritation glinting from his eyes was any indication, he planned to resume this conversation later. "She's right. I'll see you out." Patting his elbow, Maeve put one buttery leg in front of the other and led Spencer to the door. To acknowledge the scowl darkening his face would shred her last thread of composure.

"I'll be in touch," he said.

Once the door closed behind him, she rested her forehead on the cool wood.

"He's not wrong, you know." Calista pointed at the scattered paper. "This investigation you're conducting will bring nothing but trouble."

"Is this your sixth sense talking?"

"My common sense. Something you're severely lacking lately." She dipped a hand inside the tiny purse hanging from her shoulder.

"Not another vial of one of your concoctions to keep me safe."

"Just getting my keys." She tipped her head to one side. "I wish I did have something to rein in your determination to involve yourself in a dangerous situation."

Despite the towering shoes, she glided to the door

on graceful, coltish legs.

"Be careful, Maeve."

The door clicked shut. Maeve waited for a sensation of relief to descend on her shoulders. Instead, the heavy weight of dread slouched her posture. But heeding Calista's well-intentioned advice would do more harm than good. Given the uptick in recent attacks, no one was safe.

****

Maeve flopped back in the cushiony desk chair at The Music Box and glanced at the antique clock above two blue electric guitars standing amongst the growing consignment section of the school. Time to squeeze in a snack at Happy Beans.

She entered the café, and an aromatic blast of coffee and sugar whipped her into a haze of caffeine withdrawal. Delayed effects from lack of sleep settled into her bones. She swept her gaze through the small shop for familiar faces and spotted Finn.

He stood at the counter with a wide grin spreading over his face.

Dodging a few scattered chairs and avoiding curious glances, she strode forward and dropped onto a stool. "If my blood sugar dips any lower, my legs will give out."

"You're lucky. Most of the morning crowd left. What can I get you?"

Starving, she grabbed a menu from the counter and scanned the list of sandwiches. "The usual. A turkey and cheese on rye and a large glass of water."

"Comin' up." He stopped halfway through the door to the kitchen. "Hey, I dropped off your car for an inspection. It should be ready today."

On both elbows, she sprawled across the cool counter, then popped up to blow him two smacking air kisses.

"Gratitude will get you everywhere." The corners of his eyes crinkled fine lines. "Give me a second to put in your order."

She swiveled on her stool and surveyed the customers once more. No sign of Paige.

Instead, Priscilla sat solo at a table with a cup of coffee, staring at her phone.

Time to strike up another conversation. As she shuffled over, she smacked her flip-flops on the floor with each step. "Hi, Priscilla. Is this seat taken?" She gripped the black, metal chair.

Priscilla glanced up and frowned.

Her expression was clearer than a *Do Not Disturb* sign. Maeve prodded anyway. "I hate eating alone."

"I…" Priscilla scanned the room.

The lifeline she likely sought was nonexistent. Despite Spencer's best efforts to discourage Maeve's meddlesome behavior, the prospect of taking a deeper dive into the demise of Trixie's and Marjorie's friendship was too great.

"I guess."

"Thanks." Maeve plastered on the brightest smile her taut jaw would allow and slid onto the chair. Now what? These question-and-answer sessions called for a bit more planning on her part. "Order anything good?"

Before she could reply, Priscilla leaned back and allowed a teenaged server to place a steaming bowl of clam chowder in front of her.

"Oooh, excellent choice." Maeve's mouth watered. "No one does chowdah like Finn."

Priscilla added a pack of oyster crackers and stirred. "Guess I'll need to wait a minute unless I want blistered lips."

A silence thicker than Finn's chowder followed. Why, oh why, oh why, were some people so difficult to talk to? Mulling over that puzzle made thinking of something to say more difficult.

Finn arrived with her sandwich and broke the suffocating quiet. "For you, milady."

With theatrical flourish, he presented her plate.

"Thank you." Widening her gaze, she batted her best version of pleading, doe eyes. "Join us for a bit?"

After a cursory glance at the café, he shrugged. "I guess I can spare a few minutes." He dragged over a chair from another table and straddled the back of the seat. "How's it going? You ladies catching up?"

Not in the least. "We were just discussing your skill with chowder."

"You both must have suffered busy mornings to be stopping by so late." He faced Maeve. "What do you have going on with the rest of your day?"

"Noth—" A new idea took hold. "Well, actually, I thought I'd pop into Bishop's. I've heard wonderful things about their sales assistant, Marjorie."

Priscilla's head jerked up from her bowl.

Maeve pretended not to notice. "Someone told me she's a personal shopper. I'd love to get some advice."

"Yeah," Finn said. "I used to see her with Trixie. I think she was her stylist."

Finn deserved a medal for playing right into her scheme. Maeve puckered her lips and frowned. "Yeah. I'll have to offer my condolences." With batting lashes, she sat back and gasped. "I wonder if she has any idea who might have wanted to hurt her."

Priscilla darted her gaze back and forth between them. "I don't think they were on such great terms." Once again, she picked up her spoon and stirred.

"Really? I thought Marjorie was one of Trixie's few good friends." Maeve bit into her sandwich and sighed. Finn's signature spread of mayonnaise, mustard, raw honey, and homemade cranberry sauce exploded with flavor on her tongue. This spread alone was reason enough to live in town.

Making fleeting eye contact, Priscilla stirred without eating. "True. But Marjorie also worked for her, and you can imagine how that relationship might complicate a friendship. And I think the flashiest BFF in New England had a little green monster whispering deep resentments in her ear."

"Did Trixie confide in you?" Maeve lifted a brow. Anyone who'd ever seen a true-crime story on TV knew jealousy ranked as a top motive for murder. Did this rivalry run deep enough to incite a discarded Marjorie to go to extremes?

A baby girl at the table beside them began screaming. The mother scooped her out of the highchair and diverted Priscilla's attention.

"Priscilla?" prodded Maeve.

"Huh?" She flicked her gaze toward Maeve. "Oh, um, no. Marjorie stopped by The Pin Cushion. I didn't even know who she was."

A pacifier fell to the floor. The baby wailed.

Priscilla disengaged from the conversation again.

After flashing Finn a grimace, she leaned her head into Priscilla's line of view. "What did she say?"

"Just that I should think twice before taking on the,

and I quote, 'attention vampire' as a client." She removed the napkin from her lap and placed it on the table. "The next time Trixie stopped in for a fitting, I told her what happened. She claimed her former stylist spouted sour grapes. Marjorie was under the false impression they were building a business together." She stood. "Not my concern."

Maeve glanced at the still-full bowl.

"Your coat will be ready in a day or two. I'll give you a call."

Once the door swung closed, Maeve shifted in her chair. "Was that her way of suggesting this Marjorie person had a motive?"

Finn shook his head. "Don't read too much into things. The story sounded like gossip."

"Reluctant gossip. I practically had to wrestle the words out of her." She wiggled her fingertips over Priscilla's bowl. "And who up and leaves a full bowl of that creamy goodness? Totally untouched I might add. Only someone looking for a quick escape."

Finn drifted his gaze to the bowl and then up to her face. He cracked a half smile. "You're planning to eat her leftover chowder, aren't you?"

She giggled. "Don't ask questions you already know the answer to. Besides, she left without paying. Add it to my tab." At the expression passing over his face, she burst out laughing.

"Lunch is on the house."

After finishing the chowder and one half of her sandwich, she decided to wrap up the rest.

"You're still going to Bishop's, aren't you?" Finn's mouth formed a thin line.

"Mm-mm." Her mouth was still full of one last

bite.

As he stood, the chair scraped across the floor. He took her plates to the kitchen and returned holding a box in one hand and a set of keys in another. "Let's go."

"You don't need to—"

"Neither do you. Are you coming?" He strode toward the door.

Her initial hesitation evaporated. Maybe having him around would prove useful. She'd never succeeded at small talk with strangers. He could fill in any uncomfortable lulls in conversation.

Twenty minutes later, Maeve heaved open the double doors to Bishop's and took a moment to adjust her eyes. Halloween decorations? In July? Could they at least get through Independence Day before the witch hats went up? The snicker at her ear added insult to injury. She glared at Finn. "Don't you dare say this spectacle is festive."

A hand shot to his mouth and shielded a cough. "I wouldn't dream of it." His cheeks reddened.

"Let's go, Your Royal Pumpkin Spiceness."

"After you, Miss Firecracker."

Despite best efforts, she couldn't fight her betraying lips that insisted on turning up.

The escalator took them to the second-floor home of high-end fashion. Due to the scrutinizing stares from the salespeople who worked the floor, she always avoided this section of the store. Twenty-dollar jeans and a T-shirt projected frugality, not a big spender. On the rare occasions she perused the racks with Mom, she swore a probing stare waited to catch her shoplifting. No time to let those fears get to her today. "When you see her, you'll know her, right? Geesh, I hope she's working today."

Finn scanned the floor. "She's by the dressing room." He gestured toward a corner display of shoes.

Thank goodness the pricey part of the store was organized with racks placed far apart. This clothing department loomed in stark contrast to the stores she frequented. Those racks were smushed together without enough room for two customers to maneuver through at once.

One glimpse of Marjorie proved enough to form an initial impression. No one should judge a book by its cover, but the mile-high hair and glaring fuchsia lips explained why Finn described her as flashy. Moving closer, she took in the lilac dress the woman probably believed was demure given the halter neck and the fact the hem hit at midcalf. However, the material clung like a bathing suit. Teetering on four-inch heels also detracted from what might serve as a conservative style on someone else.

With shoulders back and head held high, Maeve glided toward a display of cocktail dresses and grabbed a random hanger. Right on cue, Marjorie made a beeline for her. She blinded them with a smile full of gleaming white teeth. How in the world did she keep that iridescent lipstick off those pearly choppers? And why on earth did she think a flaming pink mouth paired well with a bright-purple dress?

"May I help you find something?"

Marjorie's high-pitched voice fit her little girl playing dress-up appearance to a *T*. Maeve met her dazzling smile with a grin. "I have a function this weekend, and I'm looking for something to wear."

Marjorie dropped her gaze to the white dress on the hanger and shuddered. "May I?" Pinching her thumb and index finger to the metal hook, she screwed up her face and returned the dress to the rack. "I hope you don't mind my saying, but I don't think white is your color. With your complexion, it'll totally wash you out."

Finn smirked. "What would you suggest?"

Blue-lined eyes, heavy with black mascara, narrowed. "I know you. You serve coffee at that little place in Hampton Beach."

"Yes, I do." He shoved his hands into the pockets of his cargo shorts.

"You make a decent brew." She shifted her gaze to Maeve and lifted her chin. "You're welcome to browse. Just keep in mind our dresses are worth a week's salary for some people."

Maeve pursed her lips into a slight pout. "I know. I said the same thing to my friend not too long ago, but she insisted someone here could help me." She swept an arm up and down her torso. "I'm not much into shopping and could use a bit of advice." Working up a touch of dampness in her eyes, she fluttered her lashes at Finn and squeezed his arm. "I wish I could've come with Trixie today."

"Trixie?" A line forming between Marjorie's sculpted eyebrows cracked her foundation-spackled skin.

"Trixie Bell." Now to proceed with caution. Maintaining a calm demeanor was crucial. The mere mention of Trixie's name clearly struck a nerve. But was the color draining from Marjorie's face due to grief or guilt? Maeve tilted her head and took one tentative step forward. "Did you know her?"

Neon lips smacked shut, and Marjorie shifted in her heels. "I-I did. We were friends."

Maeve formed a wide *O* with her mouth. "I'm so sorry." She bent forward and stared at the name tag pinned to the top of the skintight dress. "*Marjorie*. I assumed she was just a customer here."

A hollow-eyed woman, shushing three clamorous children, hoisted the smallest onto her hip and slid in front of Maeve. "Sorry to interrupt, but I only have about fifteen minutes before one of these rug rats ends my errand run. Can you point me in the right direction for the shoe department?"

"Uh…um." Marjorie bowed her head, pinching the bridge above her nose. With a quick shake of her flaxen hair, she gestured toward the far-left corner of the store. "Just behind the racks of handbags."

Despite the deepening shadows under her eyes, the frazzled woman herded her trio off to continue their shopping expedition.

Marjorie faced Maeve and Finn but stared into the space between them. "When did she suggest you shop here?"

"Oh, a while ago. I haven't had a reason until now." For a moment, her mind blanked. She was supposed to be the one making inquiries. "You must be devastated. She was such a lovely person; I can't imagine who'd want to harm a hair on her head."

"Yes, I know." The department was now devoid of customers. "Uh, I need to get back to work." She gestured toward a wall display of several summery dresses. "Any of those would look great on you. Let me know if you'd like to try one on."

Heels clacking across the linoleum ended the conversation.

"Dead end." Dipping his head, Finn draped an arm across her shoulders and gave a light shake.

Maeve disagreed but kept it to herself. Sure, Finn could chalk up Marjorie's sudden urge to escape to the shock of losing her friend. But a nagging vine of doubt wrapped around Maeve's torso. Something more than grief rattled that woman.

Chapter Twelve

After an hour spent pacing the front porch with a second glass of iced tea sloshing in her grip, Maeve plunked the tumbler onto a wicker table. Finn was supposed to follow her home to drop off Jules's car but made a detour to solve an afternoon staffing hiccup at the café.

Time to pick up her new set of wheels. No more feeling like a teenager borrowing her mom's car.

He steered into the driveway and slid down the passenger side window. "Am I late?"

Incapable of waiting another second, she climbed inside, slammed the door shut, and slung the seatbelt over her shoulder. "You're early, and I'm excited."

Scrunching his face, he dropped his head to his chest and groaned.

"What?" Her breath caught.

"I forgot my wallet."

She smirked. "Very funny."

"I'm serious. I need to swing by the ranch."

Her good mood threatened to evaporate, but she forced herself to shake off the blues. A few more minutes wouldn't matter.

As Finn steered down his long gravel drive, an off-road vehicle came into view.

"Company?"

He put the car in Park and turned off the ignition.

"I'm not expecting anyone."

The house drew her gaze. "Finn? I think your front door is open."

He snapped his head toward her. "Impossible." With a clenched jaw, he followed her line of vision, hopped out of the car, and ran toward the house.

She tore after him. Only his stumble over a branch allowed her to catch up. With both hands, she grabbed his arm and yanked him backward. "Are you sure you locked the door before leaving?"

"I swear this place was sealed up tight."

"Does anyone else have a key?" The confusion on his face kicked off a throbbing pulse in her ears.

"The cleaning service. But they only come on Monday mornings at ten." With gentle fingers, he removed her grip from his arm. He lurched forward and ran up the stairs.

Every nerve ending urged her to call the police. So, why was she following him inside?

Frowning, he held a finger to his lips.

What was the point in staying quiet? Seconds ago, he pounded up the steps louder than a herd of elephants. Now was not the best time to call him out on that fact, so she nodded instead.

The clang of dishes and the hiss of bubbling water arose from the kitchen. *What burglar stops to help themselves to a mid-heist snack?* She tiptoed behind Finn through the living room, and the intruder appeared. In a whoosh of air, Maeve released a breath.

"Ryan?" asked Finn, wide-eyed.

Ryan spun with a full coffeepot in hand. "You're a sight for sore eyes. I was afraid I'd wait here all day for you to get home." He looked past Finn's shoulder and smiled. "Maeve. Long time, no see."

The dark circles under his eyes told the story of a man who'd lost several nights of sleep. "Are you okay?"

A half smile touched his lips but not his eyes. "Nope, can't say I am. Coffee?" He raised the pot.

Once they each had a full mug, Finn opened and closed his mouth. Under his thin T-shirt, his shoulder muscles tensed. "I assume you've heard?"

Ryan sagged down onto the kitchen chair and nodded. Lines etched across his forehead and down the sides of his mouth replaced once boyish good looks. The track shorts, white T-shirt, and unkempt sandy hair enhanced the image of a man struggling.

"Where have you been?" Finn asked. "Everyone's been trying to reach you. And whose car are you driving?"

"It's a rental. You know I went to New York." Ryan lifted his mug to his lips but placed it on the table without taking a sip. "This trip called for a more rugged set of wheels. That baby outside goes back tomorrow."

His words fit the context of their conversation. But the monotone of his voice raised gooseflesh on her forearms. "When did you find out about Trixie?"

"Well, I got to my apartment this morning and planned on taking a shower and a long nap."

"And when you didn't find Trixie home, you knew something was wrong," Maeve said.

"Actually, I knew she was gone." A tiny muscle under one eye quivered. "We called off the wedding before I left."

"What?" Maeve and Finn asked simultaneously.

"So, why'd you go to New York?" Finn flashed

open his palms, then dropped both hands to his side. "I thought you were looking for a new apartment."

"That was the original plan. But after the breakup, I cancelled the reservation and made a new one. I still wanted to get out of town for a few days while she took some time to figure out her next move. She needed to find somewhere else to stay in the short term." He stood and padded barefoot to the slider overlooking the deck and backyard.

Finn shot a glance at Maeve before returning his gaze to Ryan's back. "Are you planning to tell us where you've been all week, or should we guess?"

"I just wanted quiet and rented a cabin. First day there, I tipped a canoe and lost my phone." He shrugged. "At the time, I saw it as an opportunity to disconnect without worrying about Trixie contacting me. I drove home today, turned on the TV, and the newscaster was saying something about sending her remains home to New Jersey." For a moment, he leaned his forehead on the sliding glass door and released a long, hissing exhale.

More concerning than his disheveled appearance was his flat, robotic speech. Either he was in shock, or he was exerting all of his strength to keep from falling apart. Maeve rested her elbows on the table, steepling her hands under her chin. "Do you know you're a suspect?"

"I figured. Isn't it always the significant other?" With eyes cast down and his lips a tight, thin line, he faced them. "I was on my way to the police station but found myself here, digging under a rock for the spare key."

After slugging down a gulp of coffee, Finn stood

and deposited his mug in the sink. "We'll go to the station with you. I'm sure you crossed paths with enough people to vouch for your whereabouts at the time of the murder."

From the look of dread on Ryan's face, that theory was false.

Almost ninety minutes and a series of interviews later, Detective Taylor dismissed Maeve and Finn but held Ryan at the station while he contacted the staff at the campground.

If Ryan paid with a credit card, he might have been off the hook. But of course, he used cash. All the better to avoid Trixie tracking him down. Now, the only fact confirmed was Ryan's departure from town the day Trixie was murdered. Forced to leave him in police custody, Maeve followed Finn across the police department's parking lot. His phone blasted a text alert far too shrill.

He checked the message and slid the phone into his back pocket. "The mechanic is closing shop soon. Do you still want to pick up the car today?"

The passenger door swung open with a gust of welcoming warmth. *Please let him not turn on the air-conditioner just yet.* "Absolutely. The trip will take my mind off the train wreck happening in that building right now." She snapped the seatbelt into place and turned on her phone. "I need to call Paige." When the voicemail clicked on, she sighed and dropped the phone into her lap. "I can't leave bad news on her voicemail."

"Let's swing by The Music Box. Maybe she's with a student."

Minutes later, she found the studio overflowing with at least thirty people of all ages organized into groups with their instruments. Paige and Jules flitted among them, beaming like a couple of mad music hatters. The musicians took turns performing their songs and receiving praise along with constructive criticism from their peers and instructors. The excitement for the Jubilee was almost palpable.

In an instant, Paige dashed over. "Why the long face? This idea of yours was brilliant."

"I'm thrilled with the response from everyone." With a mouth filled with cotton, she swallowed. "But I need to talk to you. Can we step outside for a minute?"

Her smile disappeared as Paige swept her gaze along the room. "A minute should be fine." As the door clicked shut, she raised an eyebrow. "What's wrong?"

By some miracle, the sidewalk was empty. Had a new sensational story garnered the attention of her most-devoted reporters? Hope makes the world go round, and she was entitled to a bit of faith after the events of this week. "Ryan is back." Maeve inhaled and rested both palms on her abdomen. The action did little to quell the nerves storming through her insides. "He's in police custody."

Paige squeezed her eyes shut and brought her fingertips to her temples. "What?" On a short breath, she popped open her eyes and glanced past Maeve's shoulder. "Is that Finn?"

"Yeah. We found Ryan waiting at Finn's ranch this morning. I hope I don't sound insensitive given the situation, but we're on our way to pick up my new car, and the lot closes soon. I wanted to see you first and bring you up to speed. Ryan's questioning might impact you."

Paige shook her head. "I haven't spoken to him in

weeks."

"Just do yourself a favor, and let Seamus know you two will come clean if they accuse you of covering up for Ryan—worst case scenario." She peered through the studio window at Mom shuffling everyone's positions. If time had allowed, she would have preferred to drop these bombshells outside of business hours but couldn't risk the police blindsiding Paige with a call or visit. She knew from experience that Spencer had the timing and tact of a debt collector. Hopefully, she'd manage to wrap up the rehearsal with her usual grace. "There's more. The engagement was off."

Paige held up a hand. "That doesn't make sense. What was the point in meeting me for her voice lesson?" She covered her mouth. "Wait, it all makes sense. I didn't think much of the request at the time, but Trixie asked to rehearse something new. She said she wanted something less sentimental to livestream. We spent the whole session searching for a song to suit her limited range."

A bone-rattling horn echoed down the street.

"We need to get going. I'm sorry to drop bad news and run."

"Bad news?" Wide-eyed, Paige flung out both hands with open palms. "You really have a knack for upending someone's day."

"I know." She wrinkled her nose. "Once I get home, I'll call you."

After giving Paige a quick hug, she jogged to the car and slid inside. Sinking into the cushioned seat, she closed her eyes. "Maybe opening my big mouth was a mistake. Why cause her unnecessary worry? The police might not even interview her again."

"We both know they'll drag her into the station before the day's over." Finn pulled onto the street and offered a fleeting sideways glance. "Ryan's turned up, but Paige isn't off the hook. For all we know, they're under suspicion for having plotted the murder together."

Maeve despised the truth in his words. Barbed wire coils of despair squeezed her heart. The implications of her friends' half-truths might prove more damaging than anyone could predict. How long until accusations of a cover-up conspiracy rained down?

****

Twenty minutes later, Maeve snatched her set of keys from the mechanic, let out a whoop, and skipped across the parking lot to her new car. Laughter pealed out behind her, but she couldn't care less. Though nonmaterialistic by nature, she did appreciate certain conveniences in life, such as not asking to borrow Mom's car at the ripe old age of thirty-five. The two-year-old SUV offered all the bells and whistles available within the luxury line of vehicles but didn't hold a candle to a set of wheels she could call her own. At this lowest point in her life, she'd be happy with any jalopy advertising four wheels and a running engine. Her days of salivating over lavish interiors, sound systems, high-tech features, and a sleek paint job were on hold until her bank account and credit scores saw a boost.

"Will the old clunker do?" Finn asked.

As she spun to face him, her joy deflated, and a stab of guilt shot through her core. "Are you sure?"

"Very." He grinned.

"Give me the bill. Once I have a few paychecks

under my belt, I'll reimburse you for the car and the workup."

"Consider it a gift." His smile widened. "The car's ten years old with over one hundred and fifty thousand miles. I'm not about to charge a friend the little I'd get from someone off the street." He hooked a thumb toward the mechanic. "And Stan barely needed to touch a thing."

Whether due to relief or gratitude, her limbs grew weightless. "Maybe. Or maybe you're getting rich off all those articles you've been writing." Without a doubt, the sale of this car would have garnered him a decent amount of money. But when generosity struck, arguing with him was always a futile effort.

He raised a brow and rocked back on his heels. "Entirely possible. You wouldn't believe what *The Post* is paying freelance writers these days."

In no rush to leave, she leaned back against the car, crossed her ankles, and then her arms. "Why didn't you mention your side gig?"

"Why would I?"

"Well, your most recent article mentioned my mom's music school."

"Usually, I report on local events like the upcoming July Jubilee. But the editor called me the night Trixie was found and asked what I knew." He paused and swatted at a bee darting by his ear. "So, I offered to write a few lines with the few facts I had."

A muffled, jangling ring emanated from Maeve's purse.

"Answer it. I gotta get to work."

She stepped forward and hugged him. "Thank you so much."

"Let me know how it drives."

She smiled and glanced at her phone but didn't recognize the number. "Hello?"

"Maeve?"

The familiar, clipped voice resounded over the line. "It's Priscilla."

After the seamstress's earlier exit, this call was more than unexpected. "Hey."

"If you'd like to stop by this afternoon, your jacket is ready."

"I will. Thank you."

Priscilla disconnected the call without a goodbye.

Next stop, The Pin Cushion. Nothing like arriving to work a few hours late. Hopefully, the fact she no longer needed to share her car would appease Mom.

In no time, Maeve strolled into the seamstress's shop and scanned the empty room.

At the sound of the door chime, Priscilla popped up from behind a mannequin. She gripped the hem of a dress and clenched several pins between her teeth. Swiping them into her opposite hand, she smiled. "Welcome back." With a grunt, she grabbed a hanger from a nearby rack. "Here's your coat, good as new."

Maeve followed her to the cash register and inspected the jacket lying on the counter. "Wow. You did a great job." She glanced up. "What do I owe you?"

"Fifteen. The tear was an easy fix." After accepting the twenty-dollar bill, she handed over a five. "So, did you make it over to Bishop's?"

"I did."

"Nice. I hope Marjorie helped you find something suitable to wear this weekend."

Maeve laughed. "Not quite. That part of the store

was a bit too expensive for my taste. Marjorie sniffed out my empty wallet right away."

Priscilla lifted a dainty hand and flitted away invisible gnats. "Don't take her attitude to heart."

"Do you think Trixie made enough money to maintain a wardrobe from that place?" With her head cocked to one side, Maeve lifted an eyebrow.

Instead of responding, Priscilla resumed her kneeling position at the hem of the mannequin's dress.

Maybe she hadn't spoken loud enough. Should she repeat her question? Should she take the silence as a cue to leave? Maeve shifted from one foot to the other.

"She borrowed the clothes." Priscilla sat back on her heels; her gaze still locked on the hem. "She'd put together an outfit, pose for photos, then return every piece. Marjorie let her make the returns in exchange for wearing some of her designs. She said the designer duds were the only part of their so-called friendship she'd miss."

The last statement rang true. From what she'd learned about Trixie, the social media influencer valued people who could further her career. Once she failed to find them useful, no love was lost in kicking them to the curb. "Sounds like Trixie felt comfortable confiding in you."

She smirked. "Please, she just liked to hear herself talk. And she loved having someone coo and caw over her woes. I'd tuck and pin, and she'd rant and rave about Marjorie's delusion they'd one day be in business together. Her bestie envisioned herself as stepping out of Trixie's shadow and sharing the spotlight someday."

The silver box of pins clattered to the floor and skittered across the smooth wood. Maeve stooped to retrieve the ones near her feet and laid them on the counter.

Priscilla swept long wisps of bangs out of her eyes. "Where was I?"

"Marjorie wanted to share Trixie's spotlight."

"Oh, yeah. So, when she found out Trixie was moving, she flipped a gasket because, as Trixie said, she was no one without her."

How hostile was this confrontation? Trixie wasn't known for her sensitivity regarding others' feelings. Betrayed, with her dreams and self-esteem shattered in a single blow, was Marjorie pushed too far? "Did you agree?"

She tossed back her head and cackled. "One hundred percent. Check out a few of their posts and videos. You'll see she lived in a dream world if she ever thought for one minute Trixie wasn't a one-woman show at heart."

Suddenly, she lowered her voice as if someone else might overhear in the empty shop. Maeve inched closer to hear her hushed words.

"Sometimes, I wonder if the police should consider Marjorie. Envy is as good a motive as any. Compound that truth with seeing her dreams go up in smoke and you have a solid case."

Had truer words ever been spoken? A little bit more digging might reveal enough proof to shift attention away from herself and void the police department's current list of suspects.

Chapter Thirteen

From the sidewalk, music emanated through the windows of The Music Box. Someone played on the piano an unfamiliar, yet rousing, rendition of a song. Maeve entered on the last few notes and shivered at the arctic blast greeting her. The few audience members—Jules, Calista, and Paige—erupted in applause.

Jules glanced over, her face brightening. "I'm so thrilled with Cora's original song. She worked on it all last spring." She fluttered her fingers in the air, clattering bracelets along her wrist. "I'll ignore the fact you're late."

"Thanks." Eager to share her news, Maeve breezed inside and dropped her bag on the desk. "I'll make your day even better. Finn took me to pick up my car."

Squealing, Jules clapped her hands, threw back her head, and raised both arms toward the ceiling. "You're doubly excused then. And that statement is a huge gesture of good will on my part because we've been crazy busy here."

"Cora." Maeve smiled at the heavyset girl, not more than twelve or thirteen, sitting at the piano. A mass of curls framed her full cheeks and upturned nose. Her pretty face resembled the cherubic angels personified in historic paintings. "I heard you playing from outside. You sounded wonderful."

"She's all talent," said Jules. "Maeve, I need you to

get the billing ready for the summer sessions. Was Daphne able to bring you up to speed on the process?"

"She did. I'm all set."

"I'll see you all tomorrow." Cora closed her music book.

"I can't wait." Paige escorted her to the door. "Arrive early for a sound check."

"How did you two pull off these rehearsals?" asked Maeve. "The Jubilee is tomorrow."

"We barely had to lift a finger." When she turned, Paige winked at Jules. "We all pitched in making the calls. Most of our students already planned to attend tomorrow's festivities and have well-practiced pieces to choose from."

"Still. This invitation was the definition of short notice." Even if Paige and Mom failed to toot their own horns, their efforts and a dash of good luck paid off.

"We're going next door to grab a bite to eat. Do you want anything?" asked Jules.

The day was so busy, Maeve hadn't given a thought to food for hours. "I'd love a bagel and a cup of coffee."

Calista smirked and shook her head. "Good to know some things never change. I see you still choose breakfast fare, regardless of the time of day. And carbs, carbs, carbs."

"I always say there's nothing like sugary cereal for dinner." Surprising herself, Maeve grinned. As a teenager, she bristled at such remarks. Always a wisp of a human being, Calista's ability to consume endless calories while *trying* to gain weight frayed adolescent Maeve's every last nerve. Today, she recognized the genuine effort to crack a joke.

"No one is scheduled 'til later, so you'll have some peace and quiet," Paige called over her shoulder.

Savoring the solitude, Maeve used the time to process payments for the credit cards on file and issue emailed statements. Once finished, she moved on to researching automatic billing systems. After finding a few affordable options, she jotted notes until Mom returned, and the aroma of fresh baked bread wafted under her nose.

"What are you doing?" Mom stood beside her, holding lunch.

"Umm." Stalling for time to formulate a vague response, she tapped her scraps into a neat pile and folded her hands on top. "Just making a few notes for myself."

Jules glared at the screen and dropped the bag on the desk. "Cha Charge?"

With a sigh, Maeve sank back in her chair. "Yes, an auto billing system."

"Oh no, you don't. I'm not getting all techy at this stage of the game."

"No one is asking you to become the next software genius. But if accounting is part of my role, I'd like to have the information more streamlined. If you know the same recurring payments come in and invoices go out each month, sending bills and receipts piecemeal doesn't make sense."

With a grunt, Jules scrunched her face and planted both hands on her slim hips. "And what happens if you up and quit on me?"

"Then whoever takes my place will have a far-easier time stepping into my shoes."

"Daphne managed just fine."

And there goes the chin. She rolled her eyes at Mom's exaggerated pout. "Daphne was handling as much as she could online. She'd flit back and forth between the computer and your ancient filing system to keep the peace." Met with a dismissive snort, Maeve threw up her hands. "Mom. Her work was doubled while she tried to dredge up enough nerve to ask you to move into the twenty-first century." She tapped the screen and stood. "Try to be open-minded. If we take Daphne's efforts a step farther, the money spent will pay off."

"Weren't you the one just telling me my business was failing?" Jules dropped into the now-vacant desk chair and scowled at the computer.

"I didn't say anything was *failing*. And besides, I'll need to free up some time to focus on the new performance aspect of your school."

Jules scrolled through the screen and clicked on several tabs. She dragged her fingers through her hair and sat back. "If you insist. But I don't want to hear the first thing about any problems cropping up."

That concession was more palatable than Maeve expected. She had two wins with Mom this week. What alternate universe was she living in? Resolving not to question a good thing, she made a silent promise to herself to keep Mom unaware of any tech hiccups.

"I have a lesson to prep for." After one last tap on the keyboard, Jules stood and stalked toward the voice room.

Just then, Paige burst through the front door and hurried inside. "Oh good. Milo isn't here yet." She dashed to the piano, tossed her jacket onto a chair, sat, and rifled through sheet music. "By the way, Calista took off to run some errands. There is power in prayer, though. She arrived with the sole purpose of dousing this place in a smog of sage. *Smudging*, I think she called it. She insisted not another minute should pass without ridding this place of negative energy." She sliced an arm through the air and groaned. "The thought of suffocating in a fog of fumes for the rest of the afternoon did me in. I begged her off by saying she'd distract the students. Not to mention, who knows what allergies these kids have? Good luck to Delia at the flower shop. I think she's in for an unsolicited pitch from your cousin. More importantly, I called to check on Ryan."

Head spinning from Paige's lightning-speed dump of words, Maeve held up her hands. "Take a breath. You'll hyperventilate before your student arrives. How was Ryan?"

"I couldn't reach him, and I don't know where he is. Maybe the police are still interviewing him."

The front door jingled the arrival of two students.

"Hi, Milo. Grant." Paige stood and waved. "Come on over. This is Maeve. You'll be seeing a lot of her." Before joining Milo at the piano, Paige shuffled Grant toward the voice room.

With the last item on her to-do list checked off, Maeve had a few unexpected minutes of free time on her hands. She'd love to pay Baxter a visit and pick his brain. But, even if she could invent a plausible reason for turning up in his hospital room, she was chained to the studio. Unsure what to do next, Maeve searched for Trixie's folder. She dug through the filing cabinet, slid out the file, and laid it on top of the still-open drawer.

Nothing of interest or importance jumped out. She

pursed her lips and closed the folder. What was she looking for? As she clicked the bottom to better align the few papers inside, a small thin sheet slipped out and drifted to the floor. She picked up the copy of a receipt detailing the purchase of a keyboard on consignment and the amount paid to the studio.

The front door jingled another arrival.

Maeve glanced up. The sight of Greyson standing in the entryway, shifting from one foot to the other, sent a jolt through her chest. What was he doing here? And where was his trademark, smarmy confidence? She slid the receipt inside the folder, rushed past a gaping Paige, grabbed his arm, and dragged him outside onto the sidewalk. "What do you want?"

"I'm leaving town." As he inched closer, a line formed between his eyebrows. "But I wanted to see you one more time. Do you have a few minutes?"

Aware of onlookers, she cast her glance up and down the street. Heads turned from every direction. Recognition dawned on faces passing by. She'd had enough humiliation for one month. Fortunately, Ryan's sudden appearance drew most of the public's attention away. No need to reignite their interest. "Not really."

"My car's right over there." He gestured toward the black SUV parked along the sidewalk. "Give me ten minutes, tops."

"In the car. I don't need every ear in town listening."

After turning off the alarm, he rounded the car and dropped into the driver's seat.

Call her old-fashioned, but one would have thought he'd opt for a touch of chivalry and open the passenger door for her first—especially given the little he had in his favor. "Get out your phone and set a timer for ten minutes."

He stared out the windshield. "Come home with me."

"Time's up." She grasped the door handle, but two large hands engulfed hers. Heat rose up her neck, and tears pricked the back of her eyes. On the verge of causing a scene, she swallowed. "Let me go."

"Let me make it up to you. We had a good thing going." He released her and rubbed the back of his neck. "I don't know what I was thinking. Shannen is nothing compared to you. You wouldn't believe what that woman has put me through. She's ruining my life." He grabbed his phone and shoved it at Maeve.

A picture appeared of Shannen's beautiful face crumpled with alligator tears sliding down her cheeks. Yet, not a smudge of eye makeup marred her complexion. The gossip magazine article below the photo detailed her *harrowing* experience as a victim of *womanizer* Greyson Walker. "I'm not supposed to agree with her story?"

"Scroll."

Despite the routine Botox treatments she knew he was so fond of, Maeve watched his forehead furrow with a roadmap of lines.

"She's making a complete spectacle of herself and dragging my name through the mud in the process."

Maeve yanked the phone from his grip and read Shannen's allegation Greyson cheated on her with Trixie Bell, who was set to join his morning show this fall. She not-so-subtly implied perhaps he had something to do with her murder. His image couldn't withstand another accusation of womanizing so soon after betraying his fiancée. He had a clear motive to cover up his scandalous behavior. Maeve tossed the phone into his lap. "You don't want me to come back so we can pick up where we left off. You want me to clear your name."

The thud of his hands slamming the steering wheel shook the car. She lurched back at the finger stabbing the air in front of her face.

"You know I had nothing to do with what happened to Trixie." He slapped the finger-wielding hand onto his thigh. "If anything, I wouldn't be surprised if Shannen is behind the murder. You didn't see her that morning. She wasn't thinking clearly."

"I don't doubt it." At a loss, she opened the car door and climbed out. "I can't help you, Greyson. If you think Shannen hurt Trixie, go to the police. Either way, leave me out of your toxic love life." She slammed the door and marched back to The Music Box, almost colliding with Milo and Grant on their way out.

Paige stood behind the piano and zipped closed her purse.

"Don't ask." Maeve stopped short. Even from a distance, marionette-like lines ran down the sides of Paige's mouth. The source of her expression resulted from something other than Greyson's unannounced appearance. "What's wrong?"

"Detective Taylor called and asked me to stop by."

Her gut twisted. Every instinct screamed that Spencer would attempt to connect Paige and Ryan in a plot to get rid of his tiresome fiancée. "You need to call Seamus, and the two of you need to go in and admit you were together at the time of the murder."

Paige curled her fingers into claws and raked them

through her hair. "Stop telling me what I *need* to do."

Stung, Maeve froze. Only the remorse reflected in Paige's eyes dulled the verbal slap.

"I'm sorry." In an instant, Paige rushed across the room and squeezed Maeve's hand. The faintest tremble touched her bottom lip. "I'm a ball of nerves. And you're right. I've already called Seamus and basically told him what you just said." She clutched her teeny purse to her chest. "We should have told the truth from the start."

"Well, at least they'll know you weren't involved with Ryan or hiding him these last few days."

"I'd better go." Paige opened the door, but something taped to the top of the frame drifted to the ground. Bending, she called over her shoulder. "This envelope has your name."

"Why would someone tape a letter to the door instead of bringing it inside?" Not to mention, she was outside only minutes ago and would have noticed someone lurking nearby. Given recent events, her radar was on high alert for suspicious people and hounding reporters. Tilting her head, Maeve frowned and took the envelope.

"Couldn't guess. Maybe you have a secret admirer."

Despite her current frame of mind, Paige quirked her lips into what almost passed for a smile before leaving. As the door closed, Maeve tore open the flap. Three photographs slid into her palm. One image showed Trixie dressed in the same outfit she wore the day Maeve met her, one photo followed Baxter entering Sonny's Alehouse, and the third shot depicted her leaving The Music Box. A giant black *X* was drawn through all three pictures.

"Maeve?" called Mom's voice from the back room.

She scrambled to sweep the envelope and pictures into her purse before Jules could see them.

Jules closed the voice room door behind her. "Well, I'm done for the day. Carson will be here soon for a few guitar makeups. Can you stay until he's come and gone?"

"Glad to." With her heart about to beat out of her chest, she forced her lips to curve upward.

Every warning imparted by concerned family, friends, and community members echoed in her mind. The contents in that envelope delivered a clear message she could no longer ignore. What were the chances she could outwit and unmask the murderer before ending up as the next victim?

****

In the last few minutes before lessons began again at The Music Box, Maeve sat at her mother's desk, trying to absorb every second of stillness. Still reeling from what could only be perceived as a threat, she opened her bag and ran a hand over the offending envelope.

The door opened.

The piercing chime of the welcome bells shattered the quiet—and her tentative grip on composure. The sight of Carson entering did little to relax her swirling stomach. Like Paige and Daphne, he was a former student of the studio and still in high school the last time she saw him. "Look who's all grown up." *Please let the smile plastered on her face mask the nausea welling up in her throat.* "I hear you're a fan favorite around here. A few of our students are convinced they'll be the next big rock star thanks to your instruction."

A slight hint of pink crept over his cheeks. "Anything's possible." He perched on a stool next to several guitars. "My student roster's about to explode. In addition to working here, I received an offer last week for the band teacher position at the local high school."

"Congratulations." *Did her voice sound sincere?* If only she could shake the image of those pictures.

The door chimed a greeting to Carson's first student. A steady stream of people entered every thirty minutes. The one saving grace was a lack of drum students. Her rattled head risked cracking in half before withstanding that noise. By the time the studio emptied, she couldn't get outside fast enough. Despite the very real possibility she'd traumatized several children with horror-movie terror shooting out of her eyes in the form of blazing red lightning bolts, she was pretty sure she smiled at the right moments and came across as calm and carefree.

Desperate for a distraction, she texted Daphne and asked to visit the babies. *Ugh.* That Send key should pop up an *are you sure you want to send this* alert. One million stabs of guilt pierced her heart. To think a new mother of twins would welcome an impromptu visit surpassed presumptuous and bordered on self-indulgent obnoxiousness. And what if the anonymous photographer followed her? The phone dinged a reply.

—*COME NOW. ED IS RUNNING ERRANDS. I COULD USE AN EXTRA BODY TO HELP OUT WITH SADIE AND PIPER.*—

The sinking ship in her stomach righted itself.

Thirty minutes later, she entered the hospital parking lot and spotted Finn stepping out of his car with a giant gift bag. *Gifts.* She was empty-handed.

He waved with his free hand and strode toward her.

Would they believe she left a non-existent present at home? "I didn't expect to see you here."

"Last-minute visit." He held up his bag. "The baby gift arrived, and I asked if I could drop by."

"Anything good in there?"

"A baby gym and a gift card. But now I'm thinking I should have gotten two of the gyms."

Maeve grimaced. "I forgot my gift."

"Forgot to bring one—" One eyebrow twitched up as he lowered his chin. "—or buy one?"

Though ready to berate him for insulting her, the corners of her lips had a mind of their own, and she burst out laughing. "The babies arrived early," she groaned. "I'm not prepared."

Inside the main entrance, two women sat behind a large desk. The antiseptic scent hanging in the air was muted by traces of a eucalyptus air freshener.

"Which way to the maternity ward?" asked Finn.

"Is the new mother expecting you, or should we call?" asked the older of the two.

Finn shook the bag. "Oh, she's expecting us."

"Great. Hop in the elevator just behind us." The other woman, wearing an assortment of pearl necklaces, hooked a thumb over her shoulder. "Get off on the fifth floor and follow signs to maternity. You have a room number?"

"We do. Thanks."

Trapped inside the elevator, Maeve's ability to breathe decreased with each stop on the way up. "What if I was in labor right now? I'd be freaking out. Do you think there's something wrong with this tin box?"

"I know you have a phobia of escalators." Finn smirked. "Have you added elevators to your list of irrational fears?"

"Self-preservation is not an irrational trait." She giggled. "I don't think I could have shared this elevator with the younger receptionist. Her costume jewelry *absolutely* exceeded the weight capacity of this death trap."

He spread his arms wide. "Oh, now you want to school me on the virtues of self-preservation Miss I Can't Keep My Nose Out of Other People's Murder Cases."

When the doors slid open, a rush of relief blew through her chest. She'd choose stairs any day of the week over a mechanical contraption hovering a bazillion feet in the air. A swift dose of irritation replaced her anxiety. "You're not funny."

As they passed the nurse's station, Finn gave a brief wave. "We're on our way to 525. She's expecting us." Winking, he elbowed Maeve. "Depends who you ask."

The door to Room 525 flung open. "I heard your voices all the way down the hall." Wearing an oversized T-shirt, a pair of gray sweatpants, and a classic pair of no-skid hospital socks, Daphne hobbled to her bed. As she sat, her face twisted. "Mama's still not feelin' a hundred percent. You two gonna stand there all day? These kids only open their eyes once every three hours or so."

The sparse room was furnished with one patient bed, a crib, and what appeared to be a backbreaking excuse for a guest futon. With the drapes closed, only the light fixture above the bed cast a dim glow in the room. Maeve's heart surged at the sight of the infants nestled in their hospital crib. "Beautiful," she breathed. Tears filled her eyes. Babies never induced much reaction from her other than mild terror when asked to hold one. If she had a child of her own, she expected maternal instincts would kick in. But the perfection of these two precious creatures struck a note in her soul she didn't know existed.

"*I* think so." Daphne beamed. "And don't you dare go getting all weepy. I've seen enough tears today." She slapped her hands on her thighs. "Though I must admit most of the tears were my own. When they cry, I cry."

Finn placed his gift bag on the floor and joined Maeve. "Who's who?"

"Sadie's in yellow, and Piper is in purple. She might be in purple for the foreseeable future until I'm confident I can tell them apart. Get it? P is for Piper *and* purple." She leaned toward the crib at the foot of her bed. "See, eyes are already closed. I swear they opened a minute ago."

"Next time," whispered Maeve.

"No need to whisper," Daphne replied. "Those two sleep through anything and everything. Come sit."

Maeve followed Finn to a pair of wooden seats. "I'm ashamed to say I should have brought something. I didn't plan on coming today."

"Please." Daphne flicked a hand in the air. "I'm happy for the company. If they both wake up, you can gift me with holding one of them."

"Have many people stopped by?" Finn asked.

She shook her head. "Not as many as you'd expect. I think everyone's afraid visitors are too much trouble or worry we're too tired. Truth is, having an occasional diversion from the feeding and changing routine is more than welcome." She grabbed a cup of water from the rolling bedside table and sipped. "So far, I've seen my mom, my sister, and Tess. Tess was great. She offered to maintain my hair at home until I can get myself out of the house solo."

For a moment, Sadie fussed, but then conked out again.

"But visiting the salon is a social event," Maeve said. "You'll miss out on all the local gossip."

"True. But Tess is always good for a story or two. She had a real doozy today." She returned her cup to the table and, wincing, gingerly swung her legs onto the bed. "Said she's following the Trixie Bell story like it's part of her religion and is convinced Vic Adams is behind the whole thing."

Maeve's skin broke out into gooseflesh. The same thought occurred to her more than once.

"Why?" Bent over the crib, Finn lifted his head and cast a quick glance toward Maeve.

"Tess lives next door to Vic and Priscilla. The day before the murder, she was in her backyard gardening when an argument erupted. She assumed Vic and Priscilla were squabbling because, well, they're always in a snit about something." Daphne darted her gaze between them. "But the fence separating their yards has a few gaps. From where she was on the ground, she saw a woman with long, dark hair. And inching a bit closer, she recognized Trixie."

Breathless, Maeve swallowed to keep the frantic

excitement out of her voice. "What were they arguing about?"

"She didn't know. But Trixie kept saying she wouldn't 'sit on his secret forever'."

"Was Priscilla involved?" asked Finn.

"I asked the same thing." Daphne craned her neck for a peek at the twins and sat back. "Tess didn't think she was home. How could she stay inside listening to that racket without getting involved?"

Maeve shot a glance toward Finn. This was the second confrontation they knew of between Vic and Trixie. As if on cue, Ed's whistling arrival provided Maeve with a glorious opportunity to excuse herself. Despite genuine interest in Daphne's trials and tribulations of being a new mom, Maeve had a one-track mind. Did Vic's secret have something to do with the hidden cash in his office? Or, did he have a more sinister reason for ensuring Trixie's silence?

****

Once outside, Maeve grasped Finn's forearm. "We need to get over to the Adams' house."

"And do what?" He stopped short—every muscle in his face and neck jumping. "Do you think you'll get very far with an interrogation?"

The anger evident in the vein throbbing from his neck forced her back a step. "Of course not. But I want to look around." Though his shoulders remained tensed and his jaw clenched, his features softened. "You have an idea."

Groaning, he clasped both hands behind his head and looked toward the heavens.

"Come on, Finn. Spill it."

"I don't know why I'm even telling you about my

plans." Rocking back on his heels and lowering his gaze, he let out a short breath and dropped his hands. "I'm on my way over to see Vic right now."

"Why?" A rush of excitement streaked through her.

"I'm supposed to interview him about the Jubilee and the fundraiser. He wanted an article in *The Post* to draw more people."

"I'm coming." Without waiting for a response, she marched toward her car. His footsteps echoed behind her.

"Too weird. He said Priscilla had dinner plans, and he'd throw some burgers on the grill for us. I can't show up with an extra person for no good reason."

"The weather is gorgeous, and if he's grilling, you're eating outside. If not, insist on it. Make sure the front door is left unlocked." At the car, a firm hand gripped her elbow.

"You're nuts." Wide-eyed, he hung open his jaw. "I knew I should've kept my mouth shut."

Sure, a halo of crazy surrounded her idea. But she'd be a fool to let the opportunity to poke around Vic's home slip through her grasp. "When I can sneak inside safely, text me. I'll let you know when I've left."

"And what if something goes wrong?"

"Listen, Mr. Negative. As we speak, we have three innocent friends ranking high on the list of suspects. And my anxiety is through the roof. Have you seen my nails?" She shoved a hand under his nose and wiggled an unkempt set of chipped and gnawed-on fingertips. "I'm walking on eggshells waiting for the next chapter of the smear campaign threatening to ruin my name and possibly my mom's business. We don't have time to second guess ourselves." She grabbed the keys from her bag. "I'll park at the end of his street and wait for your signal."

What she'd do once inside the house was anyone's guess. In past ploys to garner more votes, Vic included Mom in a handful of dinner parties over the years. But the invitation never extended to Maeve. She didn't even know the layout of the home. *Here's to hoping for a first-floor office.* Until now, Lady Luck had eluded her. She was due for a change of fortune in the form of hard-core evidence clearing herself and her friends of any ties to Trixie's tragic end.

Chapter Fourteen

Parked beside an oversized weeping willow tree at the end of Vic's street, Maeve waited for Finn to let her know if the coast was clear. She followed Priscilla's advice and searched social media outlets for Marjorie's involvement with Trixie's media presence. Their names popped up in quite a few posts and videos offering makeup and skincare advice. Several video clips shared fashion trends and provided details about outfits modeled by Trixie. Marjorie was listed as the designer of several items.

She rummaged through her purse, looking for the pad of sticky notes and pen she'd taken from The Music Box. Only finding the yellow pad, she gave up and made a mental note of key details. That list consisted of Marjorie's statements alluding to her fledgling brand and style expertise. She used Trixie's platform to elevate her career. No one would find her behavior unusual, but the frequent appearances gave validity to Priscilla's theory of an envy motive.

The phone buzzed, jolting her into the present. A text from Finn appeared.

—*MOVE*—

Please let no one notice her. People in quiet neighborhoods have a habit of zeroing in on newcomers. With each step, she straightened her posture and held her head high.

Halfway down the street loomed the Tudor home. After taking a moment to catch her breath, she pushed back her shoulders and glided up the front walkway as if she visited all the time. On the top step, she swept her gaze along the street and then across the landing and double doors. No camera in sight. She tried the doorknob. After a gentle click, the sleek black door opened. With her heart racing, she peered through the crack and stepped inside.

Holding her breath, she darted her gaze across the foyer and into the rooms on either side. To the left was a large sitting room. Closed French doors stood to the right. *Bingo—the office.* The first door handle was locked, and her stomach seized. When the other door opened with ease, her knees buckled in the sweetest relief. But the tiny windows running the length of the doors offered little privacy.

Where to begin? She was a hide-things-in-plain-view kind of person, but this room lacked an ounce of clutter. First, she peeked into the desk drawers. Nothing caught her eye. A quick scan invoked a memory of the loose baseboard in Vic's office at the town hall. But a swift, yet meticulous, examination of the room's perimeter along the floorboards failed to reveal anything amiss.

On the verge of giving up, she landed her gaze on a tall, narrow bookshelf. A few inches separated the case from the ceiling. One more glimpse through the French doors revealed a still-empty foyer. With every muscle in her upper body begging for mercy, she hoisted a wingback chair and plodded across the hardwood floor. On an exhale ridding her straining lungs of air, she deposited the chair. This strenuous act would pay off in painful dividends tomorrow, but the risk of scraping the chair along the floor far outweighed sore arms. Standing on the chair, she ran her hands along the top of the bookshelf. Her fingertips brushed against stiff paper. Balancing on her toes and stretched to her limit, she retrieved a thin manila envelope.

The phone vibrated in her back pocket, setting off a pounding in her ears. Another text popped up.

—FINISH UP—

Did they inhale their food? Not daring to breathe, she slid out the contents and skimmed through a series of offshore accounts. From what she could tell, he deposited town money into the accounts on a regular basis. Before returning the envelope to its original spot, she snapped pictures on her phone of each page.

She drew a ragged breath, hopped down, and hauled the chair to the nearest wall. To carry the piece of furniture across the room again would strain the miniscule muscles already overexerted. Let Vic and Priscilla worry about how the chair moved. Another glance through the doors confirmed the homeowners were otherwise engaged. She crept out, tiptoed across the foyer, and let herself onto the porch.

Next door, Tess climbed out of her car.

Unable to breathe or pry her feet from the floorboards, she dug her nails into her palms. Did she have enough time to dip back inside?

"Nice to see you back in town," Tess called.

So much for a clean getaway.

"Thanks. I'll need to make an appointment with you soon. My hair is crying for a trim." She bounded onto the sidewalk. On impulse, she lifted her arm and tapped her watch. "I'm trying to meet my daily step goal. I'll be in touch." Nearing Tess's driveway, she plowed by with a wave.

Once holed up in the safe haven of her car, she flung herself back against the seat. If her heart rate returned close to normal, maybe her fingers would stop trembling so she could let Finn know she made her escape and would meet him at his ranch. More importantly, she needed to provide him with an excuse to get out of that house—*now*. Siphoning off money from the town was a far different crime than murder, but how far would Vic go to protect himself? For all she knew, Finn was wrapping up dinner with a killer.

****

After almost an hour of useless breathing exercises intended to stave off an anxiety-induced migraine, Maeve's adrenaline leapt into overdrive at the sight of Finn bumping down his driveway. The setting sun blazed a swath of yellow beneath a sky of radiant shades of pink and orange that should have eased her fears. But the whining hums and pings of the settling car offered more peace of mind than any picturesque view. She hopped off the porch swing and jogged down the steps but restrained herself from embracing Finn. Not letting go presented a definite possibility. "He's been embezzling money. Millions of it."

"Slow down." Placing both hands on her shoulders, he lowered his face close to hers. "Are you sure?"

"I've studied the pictures I took in his office—" She hated when her voice caught. Usually, the hitch occurred thanks to social discomfort or stage fright when public speaking. But, right now, Finn stood too close, stealing her ability to form a cohesive thought. She stepped back and inhaled a shaky breath, determined to prevent another falter in her speech. "And I can't fathom any other conclusion. Trixie must have known, and he wanted to keep her quiet."

"I'm not saying you're wrong, but a thief isn't a murderer."

"I know." She let out a short breath. "I'll share these images with Detective Taylor, and he can decide what to do next."

Paige's car barreled into the driveway, shooting gravel everywhere.

Seamus and Ryan sprang out of the car before she'd unbuckled her seatbelt and turned off the engine.

"I had a feeling we'd find you here." Paige jogged across the driveway. "You will *not* believe what I'm about to tell you."

"You look like *you* don't believe what you're about to say." A shiver ran down Maeve's spine.

Stopping at the foot of the stairs, Paige clasped her hands behind her head, arched back, and cackled. "I don't. We came clean and told Detective Taylor we were together in the studio the day of the murder." She dropped her hands to her hips. "At first, he was livid. He said withholding information didn't do anything to improve the suspicion surrounding us."

Seamus rested a hand on her shoulder. "We were subjected to another round of questioning, but this time, we didn't need to wonder or worry about what each other said or might say."

"Well, you're standing here, so the discussion must have gone well." Finn leaned against his car and crossed his arms.

"After a few hours, they said we could go home. But just as we were leaving, all chaos broke loose." As she tripped over a rock, Paige braced herself on Seamus's arm. "I heard the name Shannen Plum and stopped in my tracks. With everyone else on the floor distracted, I managed to catch dribs and drabs of what was going on."

The shiver intensified to an electric current reverberating throughout Maeve's entire body. "Why is Hampton PD interested in her?"

"Shannen was in another fender bender. Same old, same old." Both manicured hands flicked in the air. "But an officer at the scene in L.A. stumbled upon a receipt on the passenger side floor of her car." Paige paused and grasped Maeve by the arms. "The address under The Music Box lettering at the top caught his eye. Thanks to Shannen's recent noise about Greyson cheating on her with a murder victim, he recognized the town of Hampton and kept the receipt. After it exchanged a few hands, a scanned image finally reached Detective Taylor."

"For all Shannen's finger-pointing, she never once mentioned stepping foot in Hampton." Spinning his baseball cap backward on his head, Ryan scowled. "To have a receipt from the location of the crime scene was incriminating enough. But when Jules confirmed the printed details for a keyboard sold on consignment in June belonged to Trixie, that fact was magnified. Trixie must have been in her car at some point."

A tingling sensation rippled down the backs of both legs, leaving Maeve weak. "Where is Shannen now?" Well, this turn of events was one way to shift the media's focus away from her. They'd have a field day hypothesizing about Shannen's alleged role in Trixie's death. What secret, sordid tale caused a movie star to off an online celebrity?

"She was released from the hospital, with minor injuries, into police custody." Paige exhaled a long, hissing breath. "I think we'll be okay."

"I think you're right. And I'd say we could all do with something to eat." Finn removed his phone from a back pocket. "Vic didn't *once* wash his grilling utensils when cooking. I didn't dare eat the food he served with that bacteria-laden spatula and had to pretend I suddenly wasn't feeling well."

A pang of acute hunger rumbled Maeve's midsection. When was the last time she'd eaten today? The food couldn't get here fast enough. Maybe the lightheadedness due to low blood sugar impacted her ability to process the deluge of information raining down, but the story didn't add up. "I'll be back in a few. I need to make a quick call." Once inside, she headed for the guest room opposite the living room and called Greyson.

He answered on the first ring. "You've heard?" His voice rasped over the phone.

"I did." Torn between pressuring him for insider details and his personal take on the turn of events, she gave in to the unsettling notes of defeat in his voice. "Are you okay?"

After a brief silence, he sighed. "Yeah. Just trying to understand everything."

"Have you spoken to her?"

"Yesterday, before the news broke. She's probably blaming me for everything right about now. But her detour to Hampton set the whole chain of events in motion. That candy-apple-red car of hers might be the one thing that saves her."

A flash of a red car parked in front of Priscilla's Pin Cushion sparked Maeve's memory. "Was it a convertible?"

"Yeah, why?"

"I saw someone pitching a total fit in a car matching that description Sunday morning. I remember thanking the heavens I wasn't on the receiving end of the person's tirade."

"Sounds like her. When we spoke yesterday, she was full of remorse and said she wanted to get back together. But I think I'm just part of her current media game. She thrives on keeping the public interested in the rollercoaster she calls a life."

Maeve noted the edge in his voice taking on a softer tone and leaned back against the wall. "What's your gut feeling?"

"I know what I said last time we spoke. But, despite everything, I don't believe for one second she had anything to do with what happened to Trixie."

Greyson wasn't an actor, but he was a pro when it came to speaking with conviction. No doubt, he was worried. But who was he concerned about? Even if he wasn't directly linked to the crime, the connection to a guilty Shannen could end his career. "But the altercation I witnessed looked pretty intense."

"It wasn't an altercation. She lay in wait and then approached Trixie with the intention of apologizing for the outburst at the hotel. They got into the car to avoid any prying eyes. Shannen didn't need more bad publicity. And Trixie's career was just getting started, so neither did she."

"What happened? Shannen tricked her into getting in the car and let her have it?"

"I don't know. She confessed to getting emotional, but only because she wanted proof nothing was going on behind her back."

Perhaps Trixie's assurances failed to persuade her. Worse—maybe Trixie confirmed her suspicions. "Where did she go after her crying fit?"

"Home, I guess."

"Maybe somewhere along the way, someone saw her." Through the window, she watched a delivery car swing into the driveway. "Listen, I have to go. But please let me know if you hear anything else."

As Finn carried in three large bags, the smell of fried goodies enveloping the house was almost more than she could stand.

One half of a burger dripping with ketchup, mustard, and pickles later, a flood of energy surged through her veins. Tuning out the chatter, she mulled over her conversation with Greyson. After what she learned about Vic today, Shannen's guilt fell only within a realm befitting a total drama queen. Next, Maeve should call Spencer. Telling him about the envelope of photos was sure to trigger a tirade of I told you so's. And how would she explain breaking into Vic's house? What if he accused her of planting evidence instead of locating it?

****

At the rapid knocking on her bedroom door, Maeve lifted her head from the pillow. Bleary-eyed, she ground the grit caking her lashes. Between the hours spent contemplating her next move and forgetting her allergy meds last night, her head felt like a leaden balloon.

"Up, up, up." Mom pushed open the door. "Choose

another morning to loll about in bed. The Jubilee calls for an early start."

Wincing, Maeve sat. "I'm awake. I'll come downstairs soon."

Jules sailed in and paraded toward the windows, where she tugged up the shades and threw back the curtains, flooding the room with light.

Flopping back on the bed, Maeve shielded her eyes with her pillow. "Must you?"

"Nothing like a little vitamin D to get your motor running."

A faint patter of footsteps approached. "Coffee's ready. Try not to dawdle."

Seconds later, the door clicked closed, and Maeve removed the pillow from her face, then swung her legs over the side of the bed. She glanced at the clock. Six thirty. Mom was officially out of control. What good reason did she have to drag herself out of bed this early? Shaking off the last dregs of comfort, Maeve padded into the bathroom to brush her teeth, hoping the mint would provide her with a jolt of energy.

In fewer than fifteen minutes, she sat outside on the deck in her daily uniform of shorts and a T-shirt with a mug of steaming coffee and a bowl of cereal. Mom's half-eaten muffin sat on a plate next to a bowl of fruit and a basket of baked goods. High tide drifted a whispering breeze to tame an already blistering sun. She tapped her phone, and the screen brightened with one new text message waiting. Finn wanted to know if she'd talked to Detective Taylor yet. With all the goings-on last night, that call was put on hold. A small stone settled in her middle. Did she have a good reason for breaking into Vic's home on the heels of snooping through his office? Perhaps Spencer would find the pictures of offshore accounts so engrossing, he'd forget to give her a hard time. Resolving to get the conversation over with, she crafted a vague message to Spencer. Attaching the photos in a text, she typed:

—YOU MIGHT BE INTERESTED IN THESE—

Seconds after pressing Send, her phone rang. "Hello?" A deliberate questioning tone would imply she didn't know who called.

"How did you get these images?"

Or not. Apparently, Detective Taylor skipped common pleasantries such as *good morning.* "I'm not at liberty to say. But I'll tell you my theory."

"Imagination working overtime?"

In addition to customary greetings, his vocabulary lacked simple words of thanks, as well. If not for more pressing matters, she'd school him in the values of basic social skills. But her bruised ego took a backseat to the holes puncturing this case. "Isn't it possible Trixie found out? I've spoken with several people who witnessed a total of two blowouts between her and Vic."

"Several?" Silence. "Let's say you're right. Do you think investigating anyone is a good idea? Fear of retaliation isn't a risk?"

Any rational person would view the three pictures in her pocketbook as a threat. She pursed her lips. How could she broach the subject of the envelope without further inciting his unbridled annoyance?

"Hello?" he asked.

"I'm still here."

"Is there something else?"

"Sort of." The sudden realization the envelope was

left by someone other than Shannen stopped her breath. The actress wasn't in Hampton yesterday. Someone else taped the ominous photos to her place of business. Maybe Shannen *was* innocent. Still, unless Detective Taylor followed up on her idea about Vic, all eyes would return to her and her friends. But at the very least, he'd admit the absurdity of her oldest and dearest friends sending threats.

"Well? Will you explain what you mean by *sort of*, or am I supposed to guess?"

"Sorry. I know I'm stalling. I received something yesterday." Squeezing her eyes shut, she held her breath. "An envelope with some pictures was left at the music school."

"Pictures of what?"

"More like who. Trixie, Baxter, and..." For a moment, she moved the phone away from her face, inhaled through her nose, and released a ragged breath. "Me. Each had a giant X drawn through them."

"I'll be right over."

The call disconnected, and she sat frozen in place until Mom pranced outside with the energy of an over-caffeinated puppy.

Humming one of her favorite tunes, Mom snatched a sheet of paper from under the catastrophe of dishes cluttering her table and shook it. "While you were upstairs snoozing, I spent breakfast making a list of everything we need to accomplish between now and showtime. Call time is one sharp." She drew her eyebrows together. "You don't look good."

Maeve wrapped both hands around her mug.

"You're pale. Don't tell me you're coming down with something."

Mom never had patience with colds or the flu for herself or anyone else. When telltale symptoms of various childhood ailments arose, Jules always insisted Maeve was "fine" until proven wrong with a fever or vomiting. At that point, she relented and reassured herself and Maeve the illness would pass soon.

"No, no. I'm fine. Just still waking up." She forced a small smile and sipped her now-lukewarm coffee. "What's first on the agenda?" From the recesses of her brain, Jules's voice rambled at a breakneck pace. Making sense of her words was impossible. At the shrill jangle of the doorbell pealing through the house, she stilled, her heart rate increasing at warp speed to a full hammering in her chest.

Jules glanced at her watch and pressed her lips together. "It's not even seven thirty. Who'd drop by at this hour?"

"Detective Taylor."

The doorbell chimed again, and Jules raised a brow before leaving to open the front door.

While waiting, Maeve removed the envelope from her bag. Their approaching voices echoed from the kitchen. She braced herself for a double lecture.

In an instant, Jules spotted the pictures on the table, swiped the one of Maeve, and spun on the detective. "Is this little snapshot the reason behind your visit?"

Here we go.

"Mind if I sit?" He pulled out a chair and dragged the other two photos toward him. "When did you receive these?"

"Yesterday. Paige was leaving The Music Box, and an envelope was taped to the front of the door with my name on it."

Seeing Mom's tremulous fingers place the photo in his palm, Maeve froze, a sliver of guilt shooting through her.

After examining each photo, he raised his gaze. "Is there any chance Vic Adams knows you found out about those accounts?"

"I don't think so," she said.

"What accounts?" demanded Jules.

"Where did you find them?" he asked.

"Does it count as breaking and entering if someone leaves their door unlocked?" Across the table, his wooden expression answered that head-scratcher. A flush of heat spread up her neck and across her cheeks. Her quickening pulse thudded in her ears.

He sat back with a sigh and waited.

"I found a folder on top of a bookcase in his home office."

"Did you see anyone while you were there?" A muscle under one eye jumped as he inclined his head. "Did anyone see you?"

"No." She paused. "Well, on the way to my car, I said hello to one of the neighbors."

Exhaling, he blew out his cheeks. "Of course, you did."

Jules scraped out a chair from the table and balanced on the edge. "Will someone please tell me what's going on?"

Aware of Mom's increasing distress, Maeve squeezed her hand. Pounding on the deck stairs sent her heart into a tailspin.

Clad in multi-colored, zebra-patterned leggings and a lime-green tank top emblazoned with block-printed letters stating *Still Workin' It*, Ida landed on the top first. "Saw your front door open and knew you'd want to soak up this gorgeous morning. You missed out on a real soiree last night, my dear." She stopped short and batted her lashes at Detective Taylor. "Oops, hope we're not interrupting." Instead of excusing herself, she pranced over to the table and poked through the basket of muffins and croissants.

Who stops for a snack mid-workout?

"I'm afraid we're in the middle of something," said Jules. "Stop by after your walk, and you can tell me all about the party."

"Will do," chimed in Luanne. "The food. The dresses." She stepped toward the stairs, then swung around with a slight hop. "Remind me to tell you about one dress in particular. What was that woman's name?" she asked Ida. "Margie something or other." She giggled. "What a fright she was. Tackiest silver I've ever seen. She left a trail of glitter everywhere she walked."

Ida hooted. "Lord help anyone who sat in a chair after her. Their entire backside was covered in the sparkles she left behind. I wish you could have spared a few hours last night to join us." She pivoted and bounded down the stairs after Luanne. "We'll stop in again later."

"Sounds like you missed quite the party," Maeve said.

"I wanted to focus on today. Last night was nothing more than a get-together for local business owners, and I already knew everyone there. Today is about bringing in new clients." She gave a short laugh. "Although, I can't say I know who Margie is."

A spark of recognition flared in Maeve's chest.

Margie? She clamped a hand over her mouth.

With his hand forming a claw, Detective Taylor tapped the table with several sharp clacks from his fingernails. "Can we get back on track here?"

Maeve shook her head and grabbed her phone. "Give me a minute." She typed, and a photo appeared of Marjorie wearing a dress made of recognizable gaudy, glittering material. Her stomach somersaulted.

"Maeve?" asked Jules.

She placed her phone in front of the detective and clicked a nail onto the screen. "This dress, well not the dress, this cloth was in the dumpster with Trixie. I remember noticing remnants of fabric, and she had glitter all over her, too. Between the glitter and the reflections off the bits of glass, the inside of that dumpster looked like the aftermath of a wild New Year's Eve party."

In an otherwise unreadable face, he lifted one brow. "And you find it coincidental someone happened to wear a silvery dress last night."

"Possibly." She stopped and stared at the photo on her screen once more. "What I saw wasn't your standard dress fabric. I didn't touch it, but I could tell the texture was unique. It had almost a tin foil sheen sprinkled with silver glitter." She jabbed a finger toward the screen. "The way this dress catches the light is so similar. And they both made such a mess." Her phone buzzed with Finn's name flashing on the screen. He'd have to wait. With one swipe from her pinkie, she declined the call.

"So, her name is Marjorie Banks, not Margie?" With his index finger, Spencer underlined the caption featuring her full name.

"Yes. And Marjorie was a close friend of Trixie. Well, until she wasn't." Another slight twitch of an eyebrow and tilt of the chin told her she finally had his attention. "Let me show you." A quick search revealed several clips of video flaunting Trixie and Marjorie's fashion and beauty expertise. "If you know anything about Trixie Bell, you know she didn't like to share the limelight. From what I've heard, Marjorie's nose was a bit more than out of joint after Trixie accepted a high-profile job which didn't include her. Marjorie claimed they were still friends, even though I had it on good authority nothing was further from the truth."

"Marjorie?" Spencer's mouth formed a thin line. "When did you talk to her?"

She backtracked. "Not my fault. I just happened to stop in Bishop's, and she works there."

"I'm sure," he said, stone-faced.

Nothing like stuffing a foot in her mouth again. She worked up her best beguiling smile to diffuse the tension in his jaw. Apparently, she didn't know how to beguile anyone because his expression didn't flinch. "I know for a fact Trixie started taking her clothes somewhere new for alterations because they had a falling out. Rumor has it Marjorie was ready to quit her job so they could go into business together after investing her savings into building their brand—a brand Trixie viewed as her own. But Marjorie designed the dresses, paid for ad space, and bought products for them to review." She ticked off each item on her fingers. "Those were just a few expenses she racked up, only to have her dreams smashed."

"Maeve, really." With her lips pulling to one side, Jules squinted. "Do you honestly think this Marjorie person dumped Trixie's body, took a liking to some fabric in the dumpster, and snatched it before closing the lid? Oh, and then made herself a dress?"

Though Mom had a point, Maeve shrugged. "I know it sounds ridiculous. But Marjorie was notorious for wearing tacky outfits. Maybe she made the dress as some sort of a thumbing of the nose." One pathetic, gnawed-on nail tapped the screen. "She's the one on the front page of the local news today. Not Trixie."

Detective Taylor stood. "I suppose we have a new angle to consider." He picked up the three photos and dropped them into the envelope. "I'll take these with me. Keep your phone handy."

"I'll see you out." Maeve rose and followed him down the steps and around to the front of the house.

After yanking open the car door, he faced her. "Try to keep yourself out of trouble until you hear from me."

She smiled. "I've got a full day ahead. No time for trouble. Are you going to the Jubilee?"

"Depends how today goes."

"Well, if you can make it, be sure to stop by our booth. Our school's performances are a real treat." As she entered the house, she cocked her head at the click of heels approaching, which induced a flurry of activity in her abdomen. "I know what you're going to say."

"Doesn't mean I'm not going to say it." An audible huff blew from Jules's mouth as she crossed her arms over her chest. One heel smacked the floor in a rapid rhythm.

At the snapping tone, Maeve groaned and slouched against the door.

Jules stood at the entrance to the foyer. "I don't know what's going on or what you've been up to, but it needs to stop."

"I don't think you have anything to worry about. It sounds like the nice detective has a handle on things." The Herculean effort required to push off the doorjamb and stand upright paled in comparison to the ashen pallor passing over Mom's face, sucking every ounce of defensiveness from her body.

"Seriously? I had enough to think about today without worrying about my daughter getting herself tangled up in some murderer's crosshairs."

The doorbell rang, and Maeve said a silent prayer of thanks for the interruption. She opened the door to sweatier versions of Luanne and Ida. "You weren't gone long." She creaked open the screen.

"Just a few laps." Ida strolled inside.

"We won't keep you," said Luanne. "I know you've got a million things to do. We wanted to get a final headcount for our table tonight."

The fundraiser was open to the entire community from six to eight. However, people had the option of buying seats for the 8:00 p.m. dinner in the function room.

"Are you sitting with us?" asked Jules.

"I haven't given it any thought, but sure." She shrugged. "You'll have to excuse me. I need to take some things to the center."

Clad in a pale-pink robe and fluffy thong slippers, Calista traipsed down the stairs. "Does anyone know the meaning of the phrase *sleeping in*?"

"Mornin', Sunshine," Jules said. "We have too much to do today. Sleeping in is *not* on the agenda." She pointed toward the kitchen. "Coffee's ready."

"Calista, I feel your pain. Acutely. My mother's in

rare form this morning." Dodging Mom's swatting palm, she grabbed her purse and keys from the console table, skittered through the kitchen, and out the rear sliding doors. No need to take any chances of Jules stopping her.

Jogging to the car, she shivered, despite the brilliant sun dazzling from a cloudless sky. A nagging voice insisted the chill coursing through her veins resulted from something more ominous than the breeze blowing through the lightly woven fabric of her tee. How fast was the clock ticking on her unspecified date with disaster?

Chapter Fifteen

Two hours before showtime, Maeve hovered outside her closet door. "Mom, I'm perfectly capable of picking out my own clothes."

"Are you?" As she plucked through hangers, Jules glanced over her shoulder. "We need to make an impression today. One that says polished."

Jules wore a black A-line dress often reserved for more somber occasions.

"Part of your charm is never appearing too polished. Dress like yourself. I think I should go more casual, too. The bulk of your business is kids, and you look like you're headed to a funeral." She stretched an arm past her mother and extracted a simple, white, off-the-shoulder sundress. "Thoughts?"

Jules grabbed her hand. "Since you're asking, please tell me you're planning to do something about these horrendous nails. For the love of all vanity, either paint them or don't."

Wrenching her hand from Mom's claw-like grip, Maeve gritted her teeth. "I was planning to remove the color and go with clean nails."

"Well, whatever you do, do it soon. When a person doesn't care about their appearance, they imply a lack of pride in anything else. I don't want potential clients getting a gander of those talons." She glanced down at her dress and frowned. "I picked out my outfit days ago. Back to square one. I'll meet you downstairs in a bit."

No time to think of her own sharp retort or to marvel over the bundle of nerves consuming Mom. The woman made a career of perfecting the image of a composed and confident businesswoman. But today's launch of a new business idea sparked a level of excitement she doubted Mom experienced since opening The Music Box.

One peek at the time sent her hopping in and out of the shower in record time. The last thing to take care of was her hair. Instead of taming her frizz, the smoothing serum left her strands oily. Skipping conditioner to save time was a huge mistake. Maybe slicking back her hair while wet would help. She rummaged under the sink until she found a spray bottle. Another twenty minutes passed before she finagled the mess into a damp chignon still sprouting errant flyaways all over her head.

She entered the kitchen and found Jules wearing slim, dark-gray pants and a V-neck, white satin blouse. The sleeveless blouse said class, but the four-inch black stilettos surpassed chic. Once they hit the sand, bare feet would replace the shoes. Mom gave her the once-over.

"Prideful enough?" Maeve smirked and waggled clean fingernails in the air. Fluttering eyelids lifted toward the ceiling meant one of two things. Either Mom was annoyed, or she appreciated the humor. She never let on which way her mood pendulum swung.

"Calista is already in the car. Is that updo how you're wearing your hair tonight?"

"You look lovely, as well, Mother." After a peck

on Mom's cheek, she bowed her head and pointed. "But really, how practical are those shoes for the beach?"

"I'm bringing flat sandals to the Jubilee." With one hand on the counter, she bent and tapped a pointy heel. "These babies are for tonight."

Maeve's ringing phone cut short the exchange. Greyson's name flashed on the screen. "Greyson?" A resounding snort and muttering of choice words from Mom sent her into the family room.

"They released Shannen."

"Wow." How long until public scrutiny of Shannen shifted to her? "When?"

"I'm not sure. But the police are in possession of a dress with Trixie's blood."

Time stood still. "What?"

"Yeah, I don't know all the details. But a dress and the blood pointed the finger at someone else. Oh, and some flecks of glass were embedded in the fabric. I just wanted to say thanks for letting me vent last night."

Maeve registered only two words. Blood and dress. "Thanks for the update."

Although Marjorie flitted on and off her radar, the story came together, after all. Still, something troubled her.

"Maeve!" hollered Jules from the foyer. "Are you ready or what?"

"Coming," she called back. She dropped her phone into her purse in between her wallet and a card—the business card Baxter dropped in the trash at Vic's party. Was Marjorie responsible for what happened to him, too? When she found a free minute, she'd get in touch with Spencer. Hearing Mom call again, she set the house alarm. That free minute would wait.

The thirty minutes of quiet prior to the arrival of visitors flew by in what felt more like thirty seconds. The whirlwind set the tone for the next several hours. After every fifteen minutes of performances, mini lessons on keyboard, guitar, drums, and voice followed.

The beach event drew an audience far larger than they allowed themselves to imagine. The boardwalk teeming with people delivered an influx of parents and children wearing bathing suits and wielding ice cream cones. A perfect eighty-degree day with a slight ocean breeze meant no one felt rushed to leave. In addition to countless inquiries into lesson availability, Mom also received several offers for students to perform at local events.

"Ding! Ding! Ding!" crowed Calista. "Last bottle sold! Maeve-y, if you want a reading, it's now or never."

For the first time all day, Calista's flower decal in the sand was vacant. The giant purple banner with *The Sixth Scent* scrawled in black calligraphy drew a steady stream of men, women, and children swarming to her booth for fragrance readings. Each person took turns standing in the center of her giant cutout of a purple iris. She'd chosen the flower to represent wisdom. Years of teasing in good humor—and not so good humor—failed to shake her faith in herself. For this reason, she wore a single, blue iris pinned above her right ear. With her flaxen mane pulled back in a long, low ponytail and the delicate flower brushing her cheek, her cerulean eyes shone bluer than ever.

Visitors were instructed to remain still with their eyes closed while Calista circled them once. When standing before them again, she offered a free reading and a complimentary sample of the fragrance she deemed best suited to their individual needs. Not a single person disputed her findings. From positive to negative, unrequited love to potential romance, joy to melancholy, content with life to searching for purpose, she displayed a gift for pinpointing the emotions reverberating in the hearts of others. Many purchased full-sized fragrances of their choice in addition to her recommendations. And, of course, some men stopped, glad for a reason to talk to her. They left with bottles for mothers, sisters, and girlfriends.

"I don't know. I'm probably too sticky and tired for you to get a good reading." Groaning at Calista's smirk, she stepped onto the flower and closed her eyes. "Fine. Go ahead, and take a spin around my world." When she opened her eyes, Calista's expression sent her heart skittering. "What?"

"I—" She released a short breath. "Well, for the most part, I didn't find any surprises with you. I see sadness and worry but also relief and determination." She paused, her chest rising with a deep breath. "But I also feel a coldness. This chill is not coming from you; it's coming toward you."

More gloom and doom. Just what she needed. "Great. Thanks for ending my afternoon on a high note."

"Wait." With her ponytail falling over her shoulder, Calista dug into her case of samples and removed a vial. "At least, take this blend of peppermint, citron, and cedar."

"Sounds like an odd concoction." Taking the tiny sample, Maeve removed the cap and sniffed. "Wow, that's strong. Almost brings tears to my eyes."

"A little goes a long way. I know the scent is a bit intense, but I just have this feeling you might find it helpful. Mint has so many beneficial properties." With both hands, she closed Maeve's fingers over the vial in her palm. "Humor me, and take the scent. It's only an eighth of an ounce. If you never pull off the cap again, no harm done."

Not a drop would ever touch any part of her body, but Maeve slid the vial into a pocket. *Please let her remember to remove the perfume before tossing the dress into the laundry.* "Okay, I guess. Thank you." She shifted her gaze toward Jules, already packing up materials. "You better get a good night's sleep, Mom. Your phone will be ringing off the hook tomorrow."

"Music to my ears." She laughed. "No pun intended."

Paige strode toward them with a guitar slung over one shoulder and a keyboard under her other arm. "Let's get this stuff in our cars so we can eat. I'm famished."

"Where's your boyfriend? We could use some muscle with the tent." Hefting her folded-up display table to a standing position with rail-thin arms, Calista spoke the truth.

Smiling, Paige gestured to the left with her guitar-wielding hand. "Looks like he hasn't detached himself yet."

"What's he doing?" Maeve shielded her eyes with one hand. "He's been surrounded by children and parents all day."

"He created a program for kids to build their own computer games." She shrugged the shoulder strap higher. "Since opening his laptop, he's been in demo mode."

"Need a hand?" asked Finn.

Maeve faced him. "A few hands. This tent was a monster to put up, and I'm not looking forward to taking it down."

By the time the stakes were removed and they broke down the structure, fantasies of a quiet night at home with a big bowl of cereal for dinner pled for an excuse to leave. No such luck. Jules would never forgive her if she skipped tonight's dinner.

"I passed by a few times today. You had quite the turnout." He loaded his arms.

"Thanks to Maeve's stroke of genius." As they entered the parking lot, Jules shifted two totes full of music books over her shoulder.

"I had the idea. You did the hard work." Maeve grinned and took one of Mom's bags.

"Ah, what's it like to be so humble?" asked Paige.

"Pretty great." With a thud shaking the car, Maeve dropped her armload into the trunk. She glanced down and cringed. After sitting for two hours followed by manual labor, her dress was a wrinkled mess. "I wish I factored in a wardrobe change for tonight."

"Your slouching is the problem," said Jules. "I always tell you to mind your posture."

Observing Jules's and Paige's flawless looks, she wouldn't win an argument on the subject. Even Calista managed to maintain pristine white shorts which would rumple in five seconds on Maeve. "Maybe one of these days I'll start listening." She slammed shut the trunk and glanced in the back windshield. A can of ironing spray stood behind the back headrest. She always kept one on hand. An iron was unnecessary. A few spritzes and a shake later, wrinkles disappeared from most garments. With no time for a shower, the powder fresh scent would also help her smell better. "At least I'm prepared." She opened the back door of the car and removed the spray. "I'll run over to The Music Box. I might even try to tame my mop."

"Want some help?" asked Calista.

"Nah. I can manage."

"I hope we'll see you sometime before dessert," said Jules.

"Tell them to save my dinner plate." With her dress billowing in the breeze, she jogged to the sidewalk and crossed the street. Almost ten minutes later, she exited the studio. Her dress was wrinkle free, and her hair had been semi-cooperative. *Give this girl a pat on the back.* She found Priscilla on the sidewalk, struggling to hold onto a rack of clothes and a pile in her arms while unlocking the door to The Pin Cushion.

"Priscilla, let me help you." Maeve dashed next door and caught the clothes falling from her arms.

"Thanks. I started with two racks, but one of the wheels broke off the other one." She entered the shop and dragged the rack inside. "You can dump those on the counter. I hope I didn't lose anything trekking my way here."

"After dinner, I'll help you retrace your steps," said Maeve.

"You're a lifesaver. First, I need to run a comb through my hair. Do you mind waiting a minute while I visit the powder room?"

"Not at all." To pass the time, she poked through the rack Priscilla wheeled in. Quite a bit of talent dangled from these hangers. Priscilla had enjoyed a lengthy career of making alterations. Since when had she started designing, as well? Rounding the rack to get a better view of a blouse, she leaned, the strap of her purse latching on to a hook, and yanked the rack straight into a worktable loaded with sewing supplies. Needles, pins, and spools of thread rolled across the floor.

Maeve dropped to her knees. *So much for ridding her dress of wrinkles.* Crawling across the floor, she tried in vain to sweep the pins and needles into her hands. She extended an arm under a cabinet and groped for the spools of thread.

She gripped something metal. As a shard sliced her palm, she lurched back and dropped the item onto the floor. Her hand stinging, she picked up the glass. The ornate detailing surrounding the broken piece of mirror was as familiar as the antique sewing machine by the window. The mirror, framed by the same scrolling woodwork, hung in the shop for a lifetime. Hadn't Priscilla claimed she'd taken the piece home? A sick feeling settled in her stomach. With a shallow breath, she leaned forward and swept a hand under the cabinet once more, removing a pile of dust, some pins, a few spools of thread, and more shards of broken glass and frame.

Mirror fragments. Unmistakable, gaudy glitter. The dumpster. In slow-motion, she shifted into a kneeling position and sat on her heels. Her words to Detective Taylor flooded through her mind.

"Why are you on the floor?" Priscilla froze at the sight of Maeve's bloody hand. She roved her gaze over the floor and zeroed in on the broken pieces of the mirror.

The chill from this morning enveloped her in a shroud of ice. Maeve swallowed. *How to steady her voice?* "Sorry. I knocked over some things. And they rolled under…" Unable to finish her sentence, she gestured toward the cabinet.

"Looks like you found a mess under there."

Watching Priscilla's face harden into an expressionless mask, Maeve stood. "Yeah. I can help you clean up tomorrow before you open." A voice screamed inside her head to get out. "Everyone will wonder where we are." As she inched toward the door, seeing Priscilla's face contort into a forced, maniacal smile turned her legs to rubber.

"Aren't you going to ask me about the mirror?" She stepped closer. "I know you recognize it."

Maeve glanced down at the piece by her foot. "So, you broke it? I might have made up a story, too. After all, the mirror was in your family for a long time."

A small smile hinted at the corners of her lips, and she drifted blue tipped nails to fidget with the necklace of seashells dangling at her clavicle. "I wasn't the one who broke the family heirloom."

"Oh, well the story isn't any of my business." She scanned the room. Maybe fifty feet separated her from the door. If Priscilla didn't have a hidden weapon, she could plow past her. Deciding she had nothing to lose, she held her breath and ran for the door. For the briefest of moments, the exit was within her reach. Several steps in, Priscilla lunged from behind, wrapped a sheet of something around her torso, and tackled her to the floor. With the wind knocked from her chest, Maeve lay facedown, stunned and gasping for air. Some sort of fabric yanked taut, immobilized her arms. A pair of sewing shears held to her upward facing cheek glinted in the light. Priscilla's breath warmed her ear.

"When you couldn't leave well enough alone, you made it your business."

Maeve's arms seared with the pain from the full strength of Priscilla tightening her makeshift knot. She needed to keep her talking while she formed an exit strategy. "Priscilla, please listen to me." Without full lung capacity, her voice strangled. "Whatever happened, you'll be okay. I'm sure Trixie's death was an accident."

"Of course, it was an accident. I'm not some sort of murderer."

"I know," Maeve choked out. "Everyone will understand. This town never had any love for Trixie. But you?" She paused. In truth, she had no idea how people felt about Priscilla. The woman kept mostly to herself and appeared to avoid local chit-chat like it was the plague. The women of Clover Lane always said there's a fine line between privacy and unfriendliness. "Everyone adores you." *A little buttering up couldn't hurt given her current situation.*

Priscilla shifted to a full sitting position.

The movement did little to improve Maeve's ability to speak, but it eased the throbbing in her arms. "Did Trixie find out about you and Baxter?" A sharp intake of breath stopped her heart.

"What about me and Baxter?"

"Half the people in town know," she whispered. "You two haven't done a great job keeping your affair under wraps." Maeve strained to catch a glimpse of Priscilla's face. Knowing whether the woman was shocked or angry might prove helpful. "Was Trixie threatening to tell Vic? Why did you kill her?"

"First of all, I didn't kill anyone. And second, you're dishing up small potatoes."

Priscilla's matter-of-fact tone implied truth. But an innocent woman wouldn't pin someone to the ground over a few pieces of broken glass. "What else could she have had on you?" As the words left her mouth, Maeve blinked at an image of Vic's home office flashing before her eyes. The bookshelf was loaded with books on fashion design and sewing. "You and Vic share the office." She spoke more to herself but was met with a snort.

"The one you snooped through just the other day?"

Ringing in her ears ballooned into a high-pitched squeal. "I didn't."

"Don't bother denying facts. Tess dropped off a basket of her homegrown tomatoes and asked about your visit."

"I left because no one answered the door."

"Mm-hmm. Or maybe you let yourself inside. The next time you break into someone's house, try to remember to put the furniture back where you found it."

She hadn't had the time or strength to drag that leaden chair across their office again. Leave it to Tess and her flapping gums to tip off Priscilla. If she'd kept her big mouth shut, maybe Priscilla would have assumed the cleaning service moved the chair while vacuuming. Again, the cool sewing shears indented her cheek. A choking sob escaped her throat.

"Did you happen to see my husband today?"

Not that she expected Vic to stop by for a music lesson or one of Calista's readings, but the realization she hadn't noticed him in the crowd struck Maeve as odd. As a prominent public figure, he was usually seen schmoozing at every corner of an event. The Jubilee was his baby—his ticket to the community center renovation that would take his political resume to the next level. Did Priscilla do something to harm him? Or, had Spencer already used the embezzlement evidence to take him into custody? *Please let the latter be true.* A thin sheen of sweat broke out on her forehead. Questioning Vic should help Detective Taylor put together the clues and lead him to Priscilla. She just needed to hang on until he arrived. "No."

"Of course, you didn't. I received a message he's been detained on embezzlement charges."

Clearly, Spencer didn't waste time following Vic's paper trail. *God in Heaven above, please let him consider Priscilla's role in the scheme.* "You were in on it with him?"

"You really do have a hard time keeping up, don't you?" She dipped her head close to Maeve's ear. "Vic didn't know the first thing about that money."

But as town manager, did her shady boyfriend have access to the same accounts? "Were you and Baxter working together?"

"Ladies and gentlemen," she called out to the empty room. In her excitement, she jabbed the scissor wielding hand in the air. "We have a winner."

Thanks to Priscilla's willingness to talk, faint tendrils of courage sprouted. "So, were you planning to leave Vic?"

"I had my Dear John letter and divorce papers ready to go. We have enough to live on for the rest of our lives. For appearances, I was waiting to take off at the end of the month, and Baxter was preparing to give his notice for the New Year. We'd come together again for one heck of a New Year's Eve celebration. And then, Trixie happened."

"How did she find out?"

"You'd be surprised at how much in common you two had. Like you, she couldn't keep her nose out of other people's business. I guess her uninvited appearance was partially my fault. I didn't lock the door. But in my defense, she arrived before opening hours. A *Closed* sign, plain as day, was hanging outside." Priscilla slid to the floor. "She had a lot of nerve to barge in here. Baxter and I were in the back room, going over the accounts and our plan. Imagine the unpleasant surprise of finding her sitting in a chair by the dressing room with a pleased-as-punch smile on her face. She actually *complimented* me. Said she expected no less from Baxter, but never guessed I had a devious side and was impressed."

Priscilla could shout her innocence from a thousand rooftops, but she had every reason to cover up her boyfriend's actions. As an accomplice, she still had blood on her hands. "Did Baxter kill her?"

"Would you stop?" Priscilla jerked her body onto all fours and slithered her face toward Maeve. "No one killed her."

Recoiling from the hot breath hissing against her cheek, Maeve gagged.

With a shrug, Priscilla sat back on her haunches. "She demanded we pay her an outrageous sum of money to keep our secret. I told her she was out of her mind, and she tried to snatch the folder out of my hand. We got into a tug of war, and she fell into the mirror you loved so much." Her face contorted with a long sigh. "It all happened so fast. The next thing I knew, she fell onto the glass. At first, I thought she was knocked unconscious."

"So why didn't you call the police? A dumpster in the back of your own shop in broad daylight wasn't the best idea."

"I panicked. The dumpster was supposed to be temporary. Trash pickup wasn't due for two more days, so we agreed to come back late that night to move her. I jumped in myself and did a bang-up job concealing the body. Leave it to you to go trash picking. And then you couldn't let it go—fancied yourself as some kind of halfwit private eye." She pitched forward with a sneer screwing up her face. "Your skills were seriously lacking, though. You could use a crash course in covering your tracks. Leaving a Music Box pen as your calling card in Vic's office spelled amateur."

The pen. When she tripped, it must have fallen out of her purse. "Vic found it?"

"He was oblivious. I stopped by his office and found it on his desk. He didn't know where the pen came from." She lifted her chin and looked down her nose, smirking. "But I did. I told Baxter, and well, he only meant to scare you."

With blood rushing into her ears, Maeve searched for something to defend herself with. The best and closest option was a hanger. "But Baxter was attacked. He was almost another victim."

"He left Vic's party and discovered Marjorie waiting in the parking lot. Fun fact, he was involved with her several years ago. She found out about us, couldn't cope, and went into full-on stalker mode. Crazy witch threatened to march into the party and expose our affair. But in the middle of her hissy fit, she hauled off and clocked him with her laptop bag." She lifted a hand to her forehead and giggled. "Who knew a hidden laptop was such a dangerous weapon? My guess is she got scared and fled because we all know she never entered Sonny's Alehouse. When Baxter regained consciousness, he kept his mouth shut." She sighed. "What a sap. Still, everything was in motion for us to keep our plans."

Stunned by the madwoman's outpouring of incriminating details, Maeve shuddered at the cold flicker of dread dripping down her chest. "I won't say anything."

"No, you won't. Not yet, anyway."

Not yet? A flicker of hope faded in and out like a smoldering flame.

"I'll settle you into the closet in the back room. By the time you're found, I'll be sipping a plastic cup of white wine thirty-five thousand feet in the air on my way out of the country."

The closet? Even without a grown woman sitting on her back, Maeve continued to struggle for each shallow breath. "What if no one thinks to look for me there?"

"I'll make sure you're found within a day or so."

Though she'd never experienced claustrophobia, a vision of herself confined indefinitely in a tiny, dark space left Maeve dizzy. But would she have another chance to get away from this lunatic? "I won't struggle if you promise to send someone for me." Seeing Priscilla stand, Maeve inhaled a deep breath for the first time in eons. Before she had time to savor the sensation, Priscilla grabbed hold of her bound arms, yanked her to her knees, and then into a standing position.

Still clutching the material restraining both arms with one hand, she raised the shears to Maeve's face again.

No longer pinned down, breaking free became a real possibility. Seizing the opportunity, Maeve dropped to the floor. Rolling away, she untangled herself from the yards of fabric. Still on the ground, she kicked a rolling rack of clothing toward Priscilla and scrambled to her feet.

Priscilla, shears still in hand, blocked the exit and lunged.

An iron-like grip constricted Maeve's lungs. Frozen, she scanned the small space for any makeshift weapon. A primal need to survive took hold. She grabbed the gooseneck of a metal table lamp and threw it. A nightmare where her feet refused to move fast enough sprang to life. She tripped over one of the wheels on a clothing rack.

Priscilla pounced like a cat.

Managing to roll out from under her, Maeve clambered to her feet, hoisted a sewing machine from a table, and hurled the block of metal. The weight didn't allow for much leverage but gave her a few precious seconds to put more space between them.

Reeling from the blow to her thighs, Priscilla stumbled into a table. Unfazed, she plowed forward.

As sharp nails dug into either side of her head, Maeve recoiled from the strong scent of lilacs wafting from Priscilla's wrists, now brushing against her nose, while the deranged woman yanked her head forward.

In an instant, she remembered the perfume in her

pocket. Praying the vial hadn't fallen out of her flimsy dress during the scuffle, she released her grip on Priscilla's forearm and shoved her hand into the pocket. Still nestled inside, the smooth, glass bottle fell into her grip. With her thumb, she flicked off the cap, yanked out the mint creation, and sprayed the liquid in Pricilla's face as many times and as fast as her finger allowed.

Priscilla shrieked and stumbled back. This time when she hit the table, she reeled backward onto the floor with both hands covering her eyes.

Just then, Detective Taylor and several police officers burst through the front door, and blue lights flooded the street.

Maeve scrambled out of the way and crouched against a wall. As the handcuffs locked around Priscilla's wrists, any shreds of remaining energy fled Maeve's body.

****

Arbor Way crawled with police securing the area and onlookers straining for a glimpse of the goings-on behind the yellow tape cordoning off Priscilla's Pin Cushion. From where she stood across the street, Maeve had a clear view of the scene. Even without a fraction of Calista's otherworldly talents or a crystal ball, she foresaw tomorrow's headlines in sharp detail. The local news stations would have a field day with the story. An embezzlement scheme in a storybook beach town, concocted by the town manager and a well-known, small business owner married to another local official who nearly took the fall, made for an excellent front page. Tack on the recent developments that led police to an attempted murder scene where the victim, none other than Greyson Walker's beleaguered ex-fiancée, was attacked because of her knowledge of the assailant's involvement in the death of Trixie Bell, and the story would go viral.

Once again, The Music Box would make the news for all the wrong reasons. Maeve chose to believe the old adage *any press was good press*. Still shaken, she leaned against the warm hood of Detective Taylor's car. "How did you figure out Priscilla was behind everything?"

"I could ask you the same thing." He grinned. "I suppose this case is as good as closed. Our earlier conversation nagged at me all day. And the more I prodded Vic, the more clueless he seemed. Despite town gossip, I had the distinct impression he was still in the dark about his wife's affair. Marjorie waited in another interrogation room, and the pieces all made sense."

"The dress?"

"Yeah." He nodded. "She confirmed Priscilla gifted her with the dress to make amends for stealing her client and her ex-boyfriend."

"And therein lies the answer to who attacked Baxter at Sonny's Alehouse."

He glanced across the street at today's crime scene. "It hit me that Vic was the decoy. Sure, the hidden cash in his office and the records of illegal transfers pointed a suspicious finger at him. But a closer inspection revealed a chronic gambler hiding cash winnings from his wife."

A stream of sirens wailed by, blocking the view of activity in front of The Pin Cushion.

"How long 'til you figured out Priscilla and Baxter

embezzled the money?"

He clamped his mouth shut, but a hint of a smile touched his lips. "Not much earlier than Priscilla confessed all to you. A deeper dive into financial transfers exposed Malone skimming money from the top and depositing the funds into offshore accounts for himself and Priscilla. Trixie somehow got herself tangled up in their shenanigans."

At that moment, Finn emerged from behind an ambulance parked in front of The Music Box.

A sudden weightlessness swept over her. Had she ever been happier to see him? How did he get through the roadblock?

Spencer twisted and followed her line of vision.

When she met the detective's gaze, she realized he had more to say unrelated to the case.

But he stepped aside and cleared his throat. "I'll catch up with you later, Maeve."

His appeal wasn't lost on her. Another woman would expend an exceptional amount of effort to keep a face like that from the forefront of her mind. But the unwavering stare from the other side of the road warmed her from the inside out.

A shrill beep disabled Spencer's alarm, the door clicked closed, and the engine started.

She crossed the street, and wheels crunching over gravel sounded behind her.

After two halting steps, Finn took off running.

Hypnotized by the flecks of gold blazing from his eyes, she stopped and watched him close the gap between them.

Within seconds and without a word, he wrapped her in an embrace that stole her breath and buried his face in her neck.

Maeve breathed in unmistakable earthy notes of warm sandalwood with hints of vanilla and fresh-brewed coffee. The strength of his arms calmed her still-racing heart, and she allowed her body to relax under the weight of his forceful grip. A small cry escaped, and she squeezed closed her eyes at the burning tears threatening to spill. Her wall of hurt and regret crumbled. After a decade apart, he still felt like home. Perhaps, a third chapter was in store.

A word about the author...

Jill Piscitello is a teacher and author with a passion for writing and an avid fan of multiple literary genres. Although she divides her reading hours among several books at a time, a lighthearted story offering an escape from the real world can always be found on her nightstand.

A native of New England, Jill lives with her family and three well-loved cats. When not planning lessons or reading and writing, she can be found spending time with her family, traveling, and going on light hikes.

Another title by the author
Tinsel and Tea Cakes